Curtis Guy was born in South London. He has been dabbling with writing since the age of 10 but has only found that he has a real love for it in recent years. After publishing two poetry books, this is his first novel.

PRODUCT

Curtis Guy

PRODUCT

First published in 2015 by Judah Publishing

Copyright © Curtis Guy 2015

The right of Curtis Guy to be identified as the author of this work has been asserted by him with accordance with the Copyright, Designs and Patents Act 1988

This is a work of fiction. Names, characters, and incidents either are products of the author's imagination or are used fictitiously. Any resemblance to actual events or persons, living or dead, is entirely coincidental.

All rights reserved.
No part of this publication may be reproduced, stored in a retrieval system, or transmitted in any form or by any means, electronic, mechanical, photocopying, recording, or otherwise, without prior permission in writing of the publisher, nor be otherwise circulated in any form of binding or cover other than that in which it is published without a similar condition including this condition being imposed on the subsequent purchaser.

British Library Cataloguing in Publication Data
A Catalogue Record for this book is available from the British Library

ISBN: 978-0-9554732-1-0
Printed and Bound in Great Britain

For Tivon, hope to see you again someday

Acknowledgements

First of all, I thank God for the inspiration to write this novel in the first place. From the idea that came to me in the Sainsbury's car park, right through to the finished book.

Then I like to send a world of love to Natasha, my beautiful wife who has continued to support me during this process and remained extremely patient throughout. You helped me to believe in my abilities and to release my imagination onto paper.

Big thanks to my proofreaders and editors. Navlette Guy, Joanne Roberts and Michelle Mclean.

Big up to my nephews, Keiran and Stefan Guy, for your excellent appearance in the book trailer. Actors don't come cheap, so thank you guys (No pun intended)

To my fellow author Maria Lewis, thanks for your advice and tips. Much appreciated and I pray that your new novel will be a success.

Much love to my children Jermaine, Shanay and Tivon. And my step children, Tyra and Joel.

Prologue

The sound of heavy keys rattled against the cold cell door, arousing Malik from his semi-conscious state. Immediately he sat up, his body instinctively jumping into defence mode. This was not a place where you relaxed your guard; you could be shanked in a blink of an eye. Malik wasn't chancing his luck; he didn't have much to chance. He just wanted to ride out the remand and worry about his case later. He stood back against the wall, watching the butt of the key turning in the barrel.

The heavy door screeched open and a pair of large shiny boots stepped into the confined space, followed by a 6ft 4 brick house. The towering figure, shadowed over Malik, swinging the keys around his index finger. Malik stood still, unsure of what was coming next. Then the awkward silence broke.

'Simms! Looks like you're getting out.'

Malik twisted his face. 'What?'

'You heard mate ... you're getting out. Early release.'

Malik glanced up at the ceiling, almost expecting to see flying pigs.

'Fi real?'

He waited for the punch line, but it didn't come.

The prison officer tossed him a small carrier bag.

'Yeah, for real. Chuck your stuff in there and let's go.'

Malik didn't wait to be told again and hurried to pull his sweatshirt over his uncombed head. He then rifled inside a small bedside cabinet for the letter from his girl and a few other personal belongings. His hand stumbled upon a book that had been sent to him by his mentor. Before placing it into the bag he glanced over the title:

Boy in the Mirror, by Curtis Guy

He hadn't bothered to read it during his incarceration, choosing iron over knowledge and hitting the prison gym any chance he got. In his mind, muscle could overcome anyone or anything that got in his way. He wasn't having it.

Once out of the cell, the two men took a slow walk down the corridor towards the first door to freedom. One or two inmates stirred from their sleep as the officer's heavy footsteps echoed off the dull grey walls, breaking the sterile atmosphere.

At the end of the long corridor they passed Ronnie, a Rastafarian Malik had met in the communal hall. He was standing against his cell door talking to two wing officers; he appeared to be deeply upset about something. The pint-sized Rasta had come to Malik on a deeper level. He could see past Malik's stone like exterior and attempted to chip away the mortar bit by bit. But Malik was an institutionalised roadman, stuck in a fictional ghetto. He had one answer for Ronnie's philosophy which he said as if it was an anthem:

'It's all about the peas, blud!

Ronnie disregarded the statement and continued to chip away nevertheless. He saw something in the depths of Malik's eyes; he saw the spirit of a lion, just waiting to break out. He wanted to help him.

Ronnie looked over, noticing Malik as he passed.

'Aye, my yout! You ah get out?'

Malik proudly nodded. 'Yeah boss.'

Ronnie stroked his greying beard, his face serious.

'Dis place is not fi you, yuh haf fi deal wid di prison inna yuh mind ... mental slavery my yout ... mental slavery!'

The dread's words got under the skin of one of the two officers, even though he had no idea what Ronnie was on about. To him, it was something mystical, beyond his understanding. It pissed him off; he didn't like anyone whom he deemed a smart arse. He pushed a quivering finger into Ronnie's face, while his colleague held Ronnie back by his arms.

'Oi, Rastamouse ... shut it and don't say another word.'

Ronnie tried to free himself, his long dreadlocks swinging in every direction as he struggled.

'Ah who yuh ah call Mouse? Bun yuh an yuh lickle

Nazi fren dem!'

Malik felt an urge to jump in, but freedom was a short walk away, so he crumpled up his plastic bag and continued walking.

'Memba wha mi seh my yout,' Ronnie shouted, hoping Malik had heard him.

He had and the Rasta's words were already circling around in his head.

Once at the reception, they waited for the duty officer, who soon appeared scanning over a clipboard. Without looking up, he walked towards the counter.

'Name and number?'

Malik stood still, blank faced and noncompliant.

The short wiry man eventually looked up, his face reddening.

'I said, name and number ... you deaf?'

Malik kissed his teeth.

'Well, yuh coulda said please, innit ... name's Malik.'

'Full name ... come on I ain't got all day.'

Malik screwed his face to the side.

'Malik Simms, man.'

The Release Officer gave him a prod in the back.

'Have all of you lot got a chip on the shoulder? Give him your number, so you can get out of here.'

Malik blew downwards.

'You lot are just long...A3347DY. Now gimme my stuff man.'

After the last door to freedom opened, Malik sighed and inhaled the fresh air. It was just 7am, yet he could smell fresh cut grass wafting from a nearby field.

The Release Officer, watched as Malik sauntered through the gate. The middle aged man had been a prison officer for almost 12 years and had seen so many young men come and go, only to return, usually with a longer sentence for something more sinister. He teasingly rattled his keys to get Malik's attention.

'Simms ... I'll see you soon.'

Malik played deaf and began walking across the car park, dipping in the carrier for his mobile phone. He found it and anxiously pressed the ON switch. The phone came to life but immediately bleeped, signalling a low battery. He quickly scrolled to the last call and pressed the dial button. After a few seconds, someone answered.

'Kia! It's me man, I'm out.'

Kia screamed. 'But I thought—'

'Bun dat! Just come pick me up.'

His girl went quiet for a few seconds before she spoke again.

'Malik, I got some news-'

'Wot? Tell me quick my battery soon—'

The phoned died.

Murky Waters

The morning news crackled from a small radio, which was balancing oddly on a mountain of bills on the kitchen table. Jennifer sat down for her ritual boost; she needed it to get through another shift. She stirred the coffee, pausing as the broadcaster conveyed another disturbing headline:

'A 17 year old boy has been stabbed to death in South London. Officers from Operation Trident are keeping an open mind as to whether the stabbing was gang related.' 'The price of fuel is set to rise as....'

Hitting the off switch, Jennifer brought the news to an abrupt end, not wanting the headlines to penetrate her already low spirits. A steady trickle of debts had become a lake and she was close to drowning; working two jobs to stay above the surface.

She headed down the short corridor towards her son's bedroom, taking steady gulps from the hot mug. 'Malik, are you awake?' Knowing the obvious, she cracked open the door. 'Malik, I'm going to work. Make sure you call Lenny today. See if he can sort out that apprenticeship.'

'Yeah Mum,' Malik grunted, annoyed by the disturbance.

'You need to occupy yourself. Another boy got

killed over South London sides.'

Slowly he emerged from beneath the duvet.

'Dat's standard now mum, youts are getting *merked* everywhere.'

'Well it's not standard for me, it's disturbing!' She sighed, before leaving the room.

Jennifer had given birth to Malik when she was just 19, his father Trevor was sentenced to life in prison shortly after Malik was born. He had shot two men dead in Trinidad after a dispute over a shipment of drugs. Jennifer had been studying Law at Bristol University, aspiring to follow in her late Father's footsteps. Edwin Simms was one of a handful of West Indian barristers in the country. She was devastated when he passed away after a long battle with cancer.

Trevor, like most players, homed in on her vulnerability after meeting her at a nightclub and had smoothly seduced her away from her studies, claiming to be a Chief Executive of a major record label. She trusted the smooth skinned Trinidadian, but it was that same trust that assigned her to a rundown estate deep in the belly of Hackney.

The whirring sound of Malik's BlackBerry vibrated through the pillow, disturbing his sleep for a second time. He dug the phone out from beneath his head.

'Who's dis?' He said abruptly.

'It's me, Kia.'

The sound of his girlfriend's voice soon humbled

him.

'Sorry babe, man'z trying to sleep innit.'

'Listen, we need to talk about this baby. You can't keep avoiding it Malik.'

'I know, but I just come out of prison, I ain't ready for all of dat.'

'Has your mum gone to work?'

'Yeah man, she went a while ago. She came in my room, told me sum next yout got killed.'

Kia was silent for a moment.

'Look, I'm coming round, we need to talk.'

Malik rolled his eyes to the ceiling.

'Alright ... later.'

He cut the call short. Since his release he'd spent two weeks trying to smoke Kia's pregnancy from his memory.

Malik stood staring aimlessly at the broken tiles on the bathroom wall. Surrounded by dense mildew, they reminded him of everything that was wrong. The cold estate was alive with crack heads and grimy youths that reminded him of the plague of mice that came from every crevice within the cramped flat. The sodden tiles represented him and his mother, longing for a clean slate. Malik drifted off into deep thought, as the warm shower water massaged his tense shoulders. His mind went back to the prison cell, where, in one of his many moments of solitary boredom, he had roughly sketched a plan. It was audacious but the only way he figured, going over the details inside his head, until the loud bleeping of the intercom startled him.

'Cha.' Vexed, he climbed out from the shower and bounced down the corridor to answer.

'Yeah, who dis?'

'it's me, Kia.'

'Come up, innit.'

The sharpness in his voice told the world that he didn't want to talk babies. Malik was short, roughly 5'6, and surprisingly powerful. His long jaw line and goatee beard made him an imprint of his father, with the smooth brown skin to match. He left the front door open and quickly dried down before throwing on some jogging bottoms.

Kia stepped inside the flat.

'Malik,' she called out, before strolling down to the bass filled room. Rick Ross's gravelly voice rolled out from a heavy car speaker underneath the bed. Kia walked in and sat down, nudging Malik in his side to get his attention away from the tune that had him nonchalantly bobbing his head to. Not satisfied with his lack of response, Kia hit the pause button on the laptop.

'Don't try ignoring me Malik; I'm not in the mood for your crap.'

Kia was 18, petite and naturally beautiful, with no additives, apart from a tiny nose stud that shone out from her toffee toned skin. Her alluring eyes were bright and complimented her small rounded nose. They'd been together, on and off since the early years of secondary school. Whenever they'd broken up, there were always too many reasons to get back together.

Malik attempted to put the music back on, but an assertive Kia slammed the laptop shut and then pushed him backwards onto the bed before straddling him. 'You ready to talk now babe?' The softness returned to her voice after slightly losing her temper. She pressed her groin against his, reminding him of all the carefree moments that had now lined them up for premature parenthood.

The sound of a crying baby wailed in the back of Malik's mind, causing him to resent his girlfriend's presence. He pushed her forcefully to one side and reached for his laptop.

'It's dem same moves there, dat got you in dis situation,' he scowled.

Kia shook her head in disbelief.

'Malik ... 'I'm sure you were there too.'

He paused.

'Look, yuh have to get rid ah the baby ... it's all long. I got plans, yuh get me!'

Kia put her hand to her opened mouth, shocked at the words that she hoped she'd not heard.

'Oh my days ... are you serious?'

'Yeah, man'z serious still, my life's just beginning.'

'what about the baby? Malik, please don't do this.'

His face was blank and emotionless.

'It's me or duh baby, straight talk.'

The icy tone in his voice sent a chill down Kia's back that numbed all her emotions. She got up slowly, looking straight through the person she thought could never hurt her.

'… Bastard!

Kia grabbed her phone and car keys, before making her exit.

'… Babe,'

Malik shouted towards the slamming door as the vibration penetrated his chest, confirming the end of their relationship. Putting his head in his hands, the realisation of what had just happened melted into his heart like hot lava. He looked down at the worn bedroom carpet.

'I gotta do what I gotta do, yuh get me,' he mumbled.

After lamely convincing himself, he slipped his last cigarette out of the box and lit it.

Jennifer sat down at her desk and picked up the phone to call Lenny. Sipping her second coffee, she dialled the number and peeked over her shoulder at her line manager.

'Hello … Lenny, it's Jennifer.'

'Jennifer, long time, you cool?

'Yeah, I'm ok … Listen, can you call Malik and link up with him?'

'What, in prison?'

'No, he's out; he came out a couple of weeks ago.'

'What? He hasn't called me ... hold on, how come he's out already? I thought the trial wasn't until October.'

'God answered my prayers luv ... the woman who got robbed came forward and said Malik wasn't the third man ... said she made a mistake.'

'...Seriously?'

Lenny quizzed.

'Yeah, seriously. Apparently she's a journalist; her Dad's the Labour MP for Islington. That's why they wouldn't grant bail in the first place — plus all Malik's previous. But hear what happened, she was in court following some case ...'

Jennifer paused to check back over her shoulder.

Lenny clung on impatiently.

'Yeah, go on.'

'It's in the Hackney Press, the whole story ... Len I got to go, my boss is clocking me.'

Jennifer hung up the phone before Lenny could respond. With his mobile still clutched at the side of his face, he sighed heavily.

Marcia walked into the room after overhearing the conversation.

'What's that about Malik?'

Lenny looked up, his face saddened.

'Malik's robbery case is only in the Hackney Press. The last thing he needs is more attention.'

'You're joking! I just bought it. Hold on.'

His wife rushed off to the kitchen and soon returned with the newspaper, placing it on the coffee table before peeling through the pages.

'Look hun, it's here.'

She began to read:

'Journalist Katherine Peterson, daughter of Labour MP Charles Peterson has made a dramatic U-turn after admitting that she had mistakenly picked the wrong man from a police identity parade.

Miss Peterson had been a victim of a violent street robbery, which resulted in her sustaining a horrific injury to her left hand whilst defending herself against the knife-wielding thugs. Whilst covering a case at Snaresbrook Crown Court, she had coincidently recognised Nathan Lewis in the halls awaiting trial for an unrelated offence. It became apparent to her that he was the third man in the robbery that took place just yards from Dalston Station on Tuesday 9th Aug 2011. Lewis, who has a string of violent convictions, was arrested and charged and is now awaiting trial alongside Daniel Obenga and Ricardo Thomas.

Nineteen-year-old Malik Simms, from Hackney, served six weeks on remand for the alleged offence. He has since been released.'

Lenny adjusted his glasses.

'This is serious now ... Nathan Lewis is one

dangerous young man'

Marcia turned to Lenny, her face etched with concern.

'What, you *know* him?'

'Yeah, they call him Ninja; I used to mentor him before Malik. He pulled a knife on me and everything. I had to cut him off … the boy's disturbed.'

Marcia got up.

'That don't sound good … Anyway I have to rush off, I'm in Court at eleven. Wish me luck.'

Lenny buried his head back into the newspaper. 'Yeah good luck — oh, I've got a slot at that Academy to do a talk this afternoon, probably check Malik on the way.'

'Ok babe, don't forget your business cards,' she reminded him in her usual organised fashion.

Lenny didn't answer; he nervously stroked his clean shaven head, his mind clearly in another dimension. Whenever he stroked his head Marcia knew it was pointless communicating. It was only when the front door closed, he realised his wife had left. With the thoughts still fresh in his head, he switched on his laptop and sank down into his luxury office chair. His makeshift office fitted snugly into an alcove to the left of the chimney breast. On the wall, above his treasured antique desk, were pictures of prominent great men displayed in dark wood frames. After opening a new document he began to type.

Ghetto Fiction
By Leonard Grant

Deep in the hollows of Congo, Sudan and many forgotten regions across Africa, children as young as 7 years old are torn away from childhood dreams. Their crayons replaced by bullets and an AK47 rifle. These unfortunate souls are stripped away from their parents and made to watch whilst they're brutally murdered. They die inside, empathy no longer a part of them as they are trained to maim and kill without remorse. School is a distant dream that flashes through their minds but is soon saturated with dead bodies and gruesome images. Forgotten by the world, their cries are silent.

As a young man living in London, ask yourself, would you exchange your life for theirs? Would you give up your mobile phone, Xbox, your free education? Would you give up your freedom to take the place of a child soldier? If you could look through his eyes and look back at your life, would you still see a ghetto, a warzone with no way out? If you all were to stop and think just for a moment and ask yourselves, what exactly you are fighting for—

Lenny paused to answer his phone which was vibrating its way across the desktop.

'Malik ... you're gonna live long, I was going to

call you.'

'Seen ... my mum told me to call you innit.'

'Yeah I guessed that ... anyway I need to link you, before I go down the school.'

'Wot, yuh doing one a dem talks?'

'Yeah, I am going to talk about the kids over in Congo and Sudan ... just writing an article, to hand out after.'

Malik confusedly processed the information.

'Why ... what are they doing over there?'

Lenny sighed.

'You see, that's why I have to educate you lot. You haven't got a clue about real hard life. You —

'Lenny man, yuh bunning out my credit,'

Malik swiftly cut in before Lenny gave him a History lesson.

'Okay Malik ... meet me at The Dutchie at twelve, and if you turn up on time I'll buy you a dumpling.'

Malik laughed.

'You're a joker. A dumpling? I want rice and peas and everyting blud!

'Look, see you at twelve,'

Lenny said, chuckling.

Upper Clapton Road was busy; mainly with College students heading to The Dutchie for the lunchtime special. Lenny turned into the side street, hoping to find a parking spot near to the popular takeaway. After expertly edging the Audi into a mini sized space, he listened to the remainder of a Capleton tune before switching off the engine.

He locked the car and hurried past the William Hill betting shop, not wanting to be spotted by any of the many wasters that frequented the losers' paradise. They all seemed to have three things in common: Special Brew, talking garbage and 50p bets. Lenny had no more hours to waste trying to educate them about their heritage and rich history. They'd teased him, calling him the *Black Ghandi*, but he would just absorb the remarks as indirect compliments, knowing that their ignorance was just a smokescreen to cover their own inadequacies.

The bell chimed above the shop door as Lenny entered the now full Dutchie. Rich Caribbean vapours escaped from the small kitchen, teasing his empty stomach. He'd sacrificed breakfast to finish off his article and now the hunger gremlins were running riot. Behind the counter, Joyce was struggling to keep up with the orders being thrown at her by the huddle of students. It wasn't long before the plump Jamaican woman's pot of patience boiled over.

'Listen! One at ah blasted time, oonuh pickney nuh haf no manners ... ah one pair ah hand mi have.'

She paused, giving the boys a murderous stare.

'Who's next?'

An awkward silence filled the shop, until a tall dark skinned youth broke the atmosphere.

'Curry chicken and rice.'

The shop assistant folded her arms.

'Curry chicken and rice, wha?'

Realising his error, the teenager quickly corrected himself.

'Curry chicken and rice, please.'

'Yuh see … no manners.'

She cast an eye towards Lenny for approval.

Lenny looked on in dismay; it was another reminder that respect was almost extinct. He checked the time on his mobile phone. 12.15pm. Malik was late.

Joyce served the remaining students and then turned her attention to Lenny.

'Lenny, wat yuh having?'

'Jerk chicken special, please.'

He checked the time again.

At that moment the door swung open and a confident Malik strolled into the shop, sporting a white T-shirt and grey tracksuit bottoms, topped with a grey and black Snapback.

A youth of mixed heritage sprang up from his chair to greet him.

'Murkz, yuh cool?'

'Yeah I'm good.'

Malik touched fists with the younger youth.

He leaned towards Malik.

'Heard yuh got off'

Malik threw him a cold stare.

'Hold it down, yeah.'

He then turned and glanced around the shop for Lenny.

The Dutchie was a popular hangout spot, if you just wanted to grab a tasty dish or chill out in the adjoining cultural centre with its compact library and internet café. The yellow walls were heavily decorated with strong African artefacts and inspirational quotes. Soothing reggae music oozing from the wall mounted speakers, added to the mellow ambience. Malik spotted the unmistakable back of Lenny's bald head and snuck up on his mentor, grabbing him in a playful headlock.

'Wha gwaan Lenny?'

'Malik … you reached,'

Lenny turned and smiled.

'Yeah man, I had a mad morning still … girl problems. You know how it goes.'

Malik spoke with a tinge of emptiness.

Lenny shook his head.

'Don't watch that, you've got plenty more of them problems to come, trust me.'

Malik nodded in agreement.

After ordering Malik a plate of food, they sat down.

'So why didn't you let me know you was out?'

'Len, you know how Ninja goes on … I was just staying off road a little bit.'

Lenny leaned forward.

'Did you do it?'

Before replying, Malik scanned the shop.

'I ain't gonna lie, I did the robbery. I ain't got a clue how Ninja got picked out. He don't even look like me, but dat women said it was him ... I'm baffled still.'

Lenny studied Malik for a moment. He knew deep down that Malik was good, but also knew that he was battling with the environment.

'Listen! Malik, you're an intelligent yout, you know you're better than this roadman ting. Your mum loves you, Malik Simms ... everyone else loves this 'Murkz' character. I don't like 'Murkz' he's a violent hothead with no purpose—'

Lenny paused to drink some water.

'One minute you're Malik, the next minute you're 'Murkz'. Just be *somebody* ... preferably Malik.'

Malik calmly nodded.

'I hear you Len.'

He respected him and what he stood for; he couldn't have dreamt of having a better mentor.

'I want to talk to you about an apprenticeship, but before I go on to that. This Nathan, or Ninja — whatever you wanna call him — he's dangerous. But you probably know that already. Did you know his dad runs everything over Tottenham sides and is well known in Jamaica?'

Malik nodded, not sure where Lenny was going with the information.

'All I'm saying is you have to tread real careful.

You understand me?'

Lenny was clearly concerned, he'd dwelled in the underworld in his younger days and, through old associates he got valuable information on all the top dogs, the Lieutenants and the runners on the street. He used this to guide the youths he mentored away from certain family networks.

Malik began picking at his food as if Lenny's words had sucked the flavour out of the meal.

Lenny opened up his laptop case.

'Ok, here's the deal. I have the forms here for the apprenticeship, I've already spoken to a friend of mine who runs an Audi garage in Chingford; he's going to take you under his wing. So all we have to do now is secure the college side of things and you're set.'

Malik downed his Guinness Punch.

'Yeah, dat sounds heavy.'

Lenny passed Malik the papers and got up.

'I'm just going to photocopy this article and then get over to the Academy, so I'll check you later.'

He gathered up his paperwork.

Malik got up.

'Thanks Lenny.'

He shook his mentor's outstretched hand and headed for the door. As he stepped out onto the pavement, a blacked out Ford Focus slowed down at the traffic lights. Malik held his position and momentarily looked at his paperwork to appear occupied, unsure of whom the occupants were or if they had clocked him.

The passenger window slowly glided down and a dark hand reached out, waving a green bandana, before the driver floored the accelerator. Malik knew instantly that they were members of Ninja's gang, D.O.A (Dead on Arrival). Tucking the papers down the front of his tracksuit bottoms, Malik hustled back to his moped parked in the alleyway behind the shops. Feeling exposed, he started the noisy engine and squeezed on his battered crash helmet, which seemed to further encase the problems brewing inside his head.

Alone

Kia tensed as the cold jelly touched her flesh. She turned her head to face the ultrasound machine, not quite sure of what to expect. The young nurse began to glide the rounded instrument over Kia's supple stomach, gently pressing it into the contours of her skin.

The nurse could feel the tension in Kia's body and began stroking her arm to calm her.

'Just relax darling.'

Her accent caught Kia's attention.

'Are you from Poland or something?'

The nurse smiled.

'Yes I am. I'm Anya.'

Kia half smiled back then settled her head on the bed and tried to relax. Thoughts of Malik's whereabouts soon had Kia's mind drifting back to the school corridor where they first met. Malik had pursued her for months. She was different: intensely studious, with a desire to move away from the neglected monopoly of her housing estate. From the first kiss until now, she hadn't wanted anyone else.

Looking up at the monitor, she could see fragmented greyish shapes swirling around the screen. It all felt surreal and routine; she felt no attachment to the visuals in front of her.

Anya turned the monitor and brought it closer. Excited, she pointed to a roundish, semi-deformed shape.

'There's the baby's head.'

But the sadness in Kia's eyes dampened what should have been a happy moment. Her eyes began to glisten but she held back the tears.

Anya, who had studied nursing in Warsaw, was far from accustomed to London's high level of teenage pregnancies; she was finding it difficult to detach her emotions from the many girls who lay alone on the scanning bed with no male support.

'Do you want to know the sex?' she asked.

Kia shrugged slowly.

'I don't mind, I'm not even thinking about that.'

'Okay, leave that for now ... well, as you can hear the baby's heartbeat is sounding nice and healthy.'

Kia's face brightened for the first time.

'What, that's the heartbeat?'

Anya smiled.

'Yes luv.'

'Wow, that's amazing! I wish Malik was here.'

'Your boyfriend, I guess.'

'Well, we kind of split up when he found out I was pregnant.'

Kia turned her head to the side, unable to contain the tears that now began streaming down her innocent face. She felt alone, abandoned by her peers and the young man that she practically worshipped.

'I'm sorry, this thing is too emotional.'

Kia rose from the bed and fixed her clothes.

Anya handed her a red file and walked over to the sink to wash her hands.

'It's okay. I understand ... I see you on your next scan.'

Kia thanked her and then exited through the double doors.

Angela put the flame to her freshly built spliff and slowly drew the herbs into her lungs. Still in her night dress and seemingly oblivious to the sink full of dishes, she fumbled around for the remote control, anxious to tune into Jeremy Kyle. The smell of damp and weed filled the small living room, adding to the stench of stale food wafting out from the kitchen bin. 'Look at her ... slag.'

Angela cursed at the TV screen, as a dysfunctional paternity battle played out in front of her. She was so engrossed; she hadn't heard her daughter enter the flat.

'I'm back.'

Kia refused to address the woman as mum.

Without taking her eye off the screen, Angela took another draw on the spliff before acknowledging Kia.

'How did it go then?'

Kia rolled her eyes.

'Why you even asking? You don't even care.'

Angela finished her smoke and then stumped it

out in the ash tray.

'Did I tell you to go and get pregnant for that waster?'

'You can bloody talk! All you do is smoke weed and watch shit on TV.'

'Watch your mouth, child.'

'Nah, it's true. Malik's mum works, studies and goes church. She's proper.'

'I don't business what Malik's mum is doing, the boy is no good.'

Angela was already easing more sheets of Rizla paper out from the packet.

Kia turned her head, revolted at her mother's condition.

'Anyway, I'll soon be out of this stinking dirty flat. You don't do *Jack* round here. I got dreams, Mum. Even though I'm having this baby, I'm still gonna make it. Watch me.'

She stormed out into to the tight hallway and entered her bedroom, slamming the door behind her. Throwing herself onto her bed, she grabbed her childhood bear and then eased her head down on the pillow. Her room was utterly different from the rest of the flat. Like Kia it was compact, neat and well presented, with a brown leather bed, adorned with stylish scatter cushions. One wall was decorated with silver and cerise pink paisley wallpaper. On the adjacent wall were three floating shelves with her many books and trinkets. Her room was her haven, her place of peace, the only place where she could fantasize about living in a leafy suburb somewhere in Surrey.

Checking her mobile phone for a missed call from Malik, she began to accept that she had to make the journey alone. She glanced around the room and her eyes settled on a large poster of Mary J Blige on the back of her bedroom door. I can do it, she thought. Drawing from the diva's troubled past, she felt a renewed strength.

She reached up and took an Argos catalogue from the bookshelf and began rifling through the baby section, mentally preparing her mind for what was to come. She would have to give up the university position that she'd worked so hard to achieve, and eventually give up her part time job at the leisure centre. She knew that relying on her mother was an endeavour not worth considering. Angela had virtually given up on life from the day Kia's father packed his miniscule belongs and threw his keys down, before dragging his useless frame out the door. The memories of the brutal beatings, her mother's screams, the hate and the rare moments of love still festered in Kia's mind. Although painful, the memories birthed a sense of determination inside her to be the best mother she could be — with or without Malik.

A small stone cracked against the bedroom window, startling Kia from her thoughts. She jumped up, drew up the venetian blinds and peered down onto the patch of grass below her bedroom window.

'Who's that?'

An unkempt black man appeared from behind the communal bins. He was high and agitated.

'Kia, it's Carl,' he shouted as he ambled closer to the building.

Kia cracked open the window.

'What yuh dashing stones at my window for?'

'Tell yuh mum I'm pressing the buzzer and she ain't answering.'

'Look, just go bout yuh business yuh dirty crackhead. I ain't telling my mum nothing, stop coming to my house yeah. Now piss off.'

'Rah, is dat how yuh going on? Alright I'm gone! Just tell yuh mum I passed through.'

Kia presented a middle finger and then slammed the window shut.

'Dirty crackhead,' she shouted again.

Carl was one of the many locusts that frequented the flat and on the odd occasion he had tried to touch Kia in forbidden places. Kia had told her mother and was fobbed off about being too sensitive. If she had told Malik, she might as well have handed Carl his death certificate on a silver plate, so she opted for not being there when he was around.

Grabbing her notepad from her desk, she decided to make a list of baby accessories. Lil Wayne's whining voice rang out from her phone. Without checking the screen she anxiously answered, expecting to hear Malik's gritty voice.

'Hello.'

There was an airy silence, before a male voice spoke.

'Forget duh hellos ... just do the right thing, yuh get me.'

Before Kia could respond the line went dead, leaving her hanging in a nervous state. She knew the voice and she knew exactly what he meant; it was an indirect warning that was entangled with an uncomfortable coldness. The rollercoaster had just begun and she was bracing herself for a turbulent ride. Looking out of the window across the estate, Kia could see a snapshot of everything that she didn't want in her life in one gloomy picture. Sighing, she picked up her car keys and grabbed her handbag before heading for the front door.

The blood stained lift slowly trundled down to the ground floor of the tower block; threatening to break down at any given moment. Kia tried in vain to mask the pungent smell of urine, which immediately made her feel faint. She was far from familiar with the symptoms and sensitivities that came with pregnancy. Her mother had been so far removed from the whole issue that she had spent laborious nights on the internet reading blog after blog about childbirth.

Kia backed her Renault Clio into the only space available in the car park. It was hot outside and it seemed like everyone had headed to the park to enjoy the weather before it disappeared into the distance. After adjusting her sunglasses in the rear view mirror, she gently rubbed her hand over her stomach; she knew it wouldn't be too long before she would begin to show. Taking a deep breath, she exited the car and decided to head for the lake, hoping to find a tranquil spot to lie down. She needed to exhale; close her eyes and listen to nature's music. Drama was in the forefront of her mind and she needed clarity to help sort out her scrambled emotions.

On the edge of the lush green grass, a group of boys were huddled around a bench, openly smoking and playing obscenities from a mobile phone. The potent aroma of weed began to taint the fresh smell of roses from a nearby flower bed. This was the very scene that Kia had left the flat to escape from. She threw them a scowl of disagreement, shaking her head in disgust as she passed by the rowdy group.

'Yo sexy ... what, yuh don't like weed?'

The smallest member of the group proceeded to approach Kia, with his left hand buried down the front of his track bottoms.

'Yuh look good man, wot ... can I get duh digits?'

Kia stopped and scrolled the scrawny boy, disgusted by his audacity.

'You could never be talking to me, with your dirty

hand down your trousers.'

Embarrassed, the boy nervously fixed the brim of his cap and looked back at his friends for support. They simultaneously fell onto the grass, reeling in laughter.

One youth remained sitting on the bench, pulling hard on the remainder of the spliff.

'My man got baited up!' he yelled at the top of his voice.

Kia turned her attention to him, recognising Roman from her estate.

'Tell your little wasteman friend to wash his dirty underpants before he tries to talk to me.'

Roman smirked, recognising Kia for the first time. He jumped up from the bench. By now the younger youth was circling, screwing her down with intent; she had hurt his ego and he felt the urge to repair the damage.

'Yow,'

Roman shouted, gripping him by the back of his neck.

'Do yuh know who dat is? Yuh fool.'

'Get off me, I don't care ... girl dissed me.'

'Are you mad or duh weed gone to yuh head ... datz Murkz' girl.'

The boy paused, then backed away.

'Rah, I didn't know.'

Kia was now looking him dead in his eye.

'Got anything else you wanna say?'

'... Sorry innit, I didn't know who you were.'

Even though she was no longer with Malik, most people knew that Kia was his girl and that gave her security, which she sometimes used to her advantage.

Putting his hands up in surrender, the youth known as 'Sticky' crawled back to where he came from; leaving Roman to reason with Kia.

'Sorry bout dat, my man's an idiot, needs to stick to teefing mopeds.'

He laughed and touched fists with Kia.

Kia adjusted her sunglasses.

'It's cool; I was just playing with him anyway.'

Roman had not long been released from prison and was sporting his tag in full view, below his three quarter length jean shorts. His eyes were glazed and red, but this didn't detract Kia from noticing the deep scar on the left side of his neck.

'Look, I best go. Thanks.'

'Alright, cool ... take it easy.'

Roman placed his hand on her shoulder as a reassurance.

Leaving the reminder of her estate on the bench, Kia continued down the winding path towards the lake, anxious to find a solitary place to sit down. The playground was overflowing with energised children, who were happily darting from one apparatus to the next. She took a shortcut between the tennis courts and deliberately avoided the basketball court, not wanting to draw any further attention to her shapely figure.

After a short walk down the gravel path, the lake came into view. The surrounding grass was freshly cut and apart from the wildlife, the lakeside was fairly quiet, considering the mass of people occupying the green space.

Kia found a shaded spot underneath a huge oak tree and sat down. Just behind her, a family were quietly having an intimate barbecue. The smoky smell of chicken, teased Kia's already sensitive nostrils, reminding her that she hadn't eaten since her morning hospital appointment.

Looking out over the lake, a sense of peace replaced the emotional turmoil that was churning in the pits of her stomach.

But the peaceful ease didn't last long as a duck waddled past just a few yards in front of her with half a dozen ducklings in tow. As they entered into the shallows and began to glide across the still water, the dam that had been holding back Kia's tears for most of the day broke. The visual of nature and motherhood touched a place in her heart that she didn't even know she had. Tears began to stream from her eyes, leaving wet blotches on her white leggings. She removed her glasses and searched her handbag for a tissue. She was so embroiled in her own sorry state that she hadn't noticed the elderly lady standing beside her.

'Hey, look ah tissue.'

She handed Kia a sheet of kitchen towel and sat down next to her.

Kia dabbed the moisture from her eyes.

'Thank you.'

Turning to Kia, she placed her left hand onto her knee.

'Yuh pregnant?'

Kia paused, puzzled as to whether it was a question or a statement.

'Yes I am ... how come you said that?'

Half smiling, she gently touched Kia's face with her other hand.

'Listen child ... mi come here from Jamaica as a young girl, pretty just like you. Mi had mi first chile at 16 and den four more hafta dat. Mi husband run up and down until sex nearly kill him backside ... mi raise all mi children dem, by mi self. And den one day, God sen ah godly man into mi life and – bwoy! From den, everyting sweet like mango. Don't worry yuhself; just pray ah morning and pray ah night. Everyting will work out.'

Kia studied the old woman intently, absorbing every wrinkle on her face like a sacred book. She took the paper towel from Kia's hand.

'So where's di young man? 'I bet him run garn lef you.'

Kia sniffed.

'Yeah, he has ... well sort of.'

'Look chile ... yuh young and beautiful. Mek him gwaan bout him business.'

Kia laughed and it felt good.

The old lady fixed her wicker hat and then struggled to her feet.

'Look, we ah barbecue sum chicken, one ah mi daughter and mi grandchild dem ... come eat sum food.'

Surprised, Kia looked up.

'Are you sure?'

'Arf course mi sure darling. Remember, it's two mout yuh ah feed now.'

Kia paused, slightly puzzled.

'Oh ... yeah.' She laughed again.

The old woman's wise words had warmed her heart and put her in a more jovial mood. She felt ready to be a mother, despite the lack of support from her own and Malik. Kia brushed the loose cut grass off her leggings and went to join the family.

Original Gangster

The weather had taken a fashionable British turn, with the temperature dropping nearly ten degrees. Malik fixed his hood and put his headphones in his ears. The rush hour traffic was backed up along the Chingford Road heading south, but more so than usual due to yet more road works, more temporary traffic lights and no workmen in sight.

A group of school children dodged between the stationary cars and the oncoming traffic to catch the bus. Malik pressed the play button on his iPod and let the heavy grime tune bang his ear drums. It was 8.12am; he hated mornings, especially cold ones where he had the task of hard labour for little reward. But he owed it to Lenny; the man had put his upstanding reputation on the line for him. He couldn't forget that so easily.

Ducking into the corner shop, Malik grabbed a can of Nourishment for breakfast and hurriedly walked up the side street towards the garage. He was only a couple of weeks into his apprenticeship but was already struggling to see the long term goal. Money was scarce and the pressure was heavy, heavy enough to have him scanning over his plans to carry out the move he had planned in prison.

Ace Audi Centre sat snugly underneath some

railway arches. Malik crossed over the cobbled path and then cautiously ducked under the shutter, hoping Tony wouldn't notice him slipping in unannounced. But he was a sharp, always-on-the-ball type of man; he didn't miss anything.

'Late again mate?'

The boss's heavy voice echoed out from underneath a car bonnet.

'There's a new battery in my office, put it in that silver A3 ... the geezer's coming to pick it up at lunchtime.'

Tony's head remained buried in the engine as he barked instructions at Malik. Malik downed his breakfast, readying himself for the day's graft.

Tony emerged from under the car and waved a sizeable spanner at Malik.

'We'll talk about your lateness later ... alright?'

His imposing demeanour made Malik feel small, despite his street credentials. Tony's huge hands were heavily scarred from hard work and other inglorious activities that he didn't care to share. Malik had watched enough East End gangster films to recognise something in his boss that was shielding a dark past. With all these thoughts in mind, fitting the car battery suddenly became a priority. Malik jumped into his crisp new overalls, which were still relatively clean, with the fold

creases from the packet still clearly visible. He longed for that seasoned mechanic look, but the overalls showed everyone he was a trainee. After hoisting the heavy battery out from the office, Malik shuffled over to the silver Audi and popped the bonnet.

'Tony! What size spanner to do duh battery?'

'What, you forgotten already? ... Ten mil.'

'Thanks, Boss.'

Malik strolled over to the tool chest.

Heart FM filtered out from an old radio sitting on a stack of old tyres in the corner of the workshop. Eric Clapton's 'Watch Yourself' flowed out through the small speakers. Malik felt uneasy and slightly irritated. His ears were so used to harsh volatile beats that the mellow tones of the song made him feel out of sync.

Tony stood in the background happily humming the chorus as he adjusted the settings on the emissions machine. For the first time Malik saw a more gentle side to his boss's hard man exterior, a side he was beginning to think didn't exist.

He glanced over, admiring the Audi R8 which simply outclassed everything in the garage. Tony was busy fine tuning the engine in preparation for collection. The pearl white paintwork and black sport rims drew Malik's eyes all over its sublime curves. He'd never been so up close and personal with such a classy car.

'Nice car, Boss.'

Tony gently closed the heavy bonnet to reveal

a black carbon finish that contrasted perfectly with the main colour.

'What, you like it?'

Malik circled around the car.

'Car's maaaad, come like 'Fast n Furious.''

Tony grinned.

'Lovely innit.'

'Yeah man, dis is heavy.'

'Heavy?' Tony paused. 'Of course it's bloody heavy, you seen the size of the engine?'

'Nah, I mean bad ... you know. Duh car's phat!' Malik laughed.

Tony threw him a confused look.

'I don't get all dat mumbo jumbo ... Cockney and English, that's all I know mate.'

The door to the main workshop swung open. Zoe, Tony's new receptionist, popped her head around.

'Tony, you wanna cuppa?'

'Yes please, luv.'

'What about you, Malik?'

She deliberately flicked back her blonde hair to reveal her piercing blue eyes. Malik shook his head dismissively.

'Nah thanks, I don't really drink tea.'

'Ok, suit yourself.'

Disappointed, she headed towards the kitchen, which was situated down a narrow corridor to the side of the reception. Malik was a novelty; he was the first black guy she'd been in touching distance of. Until recently she'd lived a sheltered life with her father in a small village in Colchester, and spent most of her spare time at the stables taking care of her horses. When Tony put the word out for a receptionist, his good friend and ex villain put his daughter forward. She was perfect: young and stunning with all the attributes to keep the punters coming.

Malik glanced up at the posters of topless girls that were pasted on the back wall of the garage. He chuckled to himself, figuring exactly why Tony had employed Zoe. He finished bolting the battery in place and closed the bonnet.

'Wot next Boss?'

Tony handed him a leather cloth and a tin of formula.

'Just give the wheels on the R8 a once over and then me and you are gonna go for a little drive.'

Zoe soon returned with a mug of tea and handed it to Tony, glancing at Malik, before turning back towards the office.

Tony nudged Malik.

'Nice little arse aye?'

Malik glanced up, hardly amused.

'She's alright.'

'What do you mean, she's alright?'

Malik leaned over to continue buffing the rims.

'Where I live is pure black girls innit ... there ain't many white girls round my endz, yuh get me.'

Tony paused.

'Yeah, but she's got a bit a class— high heels, the lot.'

'What yuh saying Boss ... black girls ain't got class?'

'Nah mate, just saying a bit of etiquette on your side can take you places.'

Malik kind of got what he meant, but was still offended by his remarks.

Tony sensed it.

'Anyway, don't even think about touching that. Her old man will chop your hands off.'

Malik perked up.

'What, yuh know her dad?'

'Know him?' Tony laughed. 'I used to rob banks with the crazy bastard.'

Malik's eyes widened.

'Rah, dat's deep ... did you ever get caught?'

Tony paused and opened the door to the R8.

'Look, get in the car; we'll talk on the way.'

Malik didn't wait for a second invite and slid into the passenger seat. Tony adjusted the driver's seat to accommodate his large frame and squeezed into the confined cabin. Malik ran his fingers over the sleek black and chrome dashboard.

'Dis is niiiiice.'

Tony fixed the rear view mirror, briefly admiring his newly acquired tan. He had not long returned from a holiday in Cyprus with his wife and two children.

He watched Malik's admiration for a few seconds. 'Everything on this car is upgraded and customized. The geezer's got money to burn, mate. I've added more BHP on it, upgraded the exhaust system ... not like it needed it, the works. Car's only three months old.'

Malik put his hand to his chin and shook his head.

'Nah man, I gotta be pushing one of these.'

Tony started the car and pushed down sharply on the accelerator, sending the rev counters round the dial. The roar from the V10 engine vibrated through Malik's chest, giving him a hesitant thrill. He smoothly slotted the gearstick into reverse, before carefully backing out through the shutters. He then coasted down to the main road, and indicated right. Once on the Chingford Road, he headed north out of town.

Malik got comfortable.

'Where we heading, Boss?'

Tony stayed focused on the road ahead. He didn't like too many questions; it reminded him of the Old Bill.

'Let's just call it an educational tour.'

The big man spoke almost robotically. His chiselled features stood out from the tan glaze which accentuated the jagged scar on his right cheekbone, and his twisted, clearly broken nose.

Malik studied his boss's battle worn face, almost

in awe. He sensed that there was something sinister about the man in the driving seat, something that made him feel a level of excitement and fear at the same time. Real gangsters were just fictional characters that he could switch off with a remote control, not sit next to in the passenger seat.

Malik slouched in the seat to appear relaxed, and took a pack of cigarettes out from his inner pocket.

'Can I smoke, Boss?'

'Yeah, just ease the window down a bit.'

He held the pack in Tony's direction.

'Yuh smoke?'

Tony shook his head.

'Nah mate, gave up years ago, it was slowing me down.'

Malik lit up and then took a deep drag from the fag, which made him feel a tinge of guilt.

Tony gave the car a bit more juice and shifted through the open road for several miles, then turned down a narrow lane. Malik engrossed himself in the scenery. It was almost alien to him; the concrete that he was so used to had disappeared miles back.

'Rah, dis is country. Where are we Boss?'

'Epping Forest mate, you know it?'

'Nah man, I ain't been out these sides before. To be honest, I ain't really left Hackney.'

Malik nervously finished the cigarette. He had heard stories about dead bodies turning up in the back of cars in the middle of nowhere and Tony looked like the type of man who would snuff someone out, then go home and read bedtime stories to his kids. After turning into a quiet private road, Tony pulled over.

'What do you mean you've never left Hackney? You see that's half the problem with you youngsters; stuck in those bloody estates, talking all this gangster crap. Don't leave the manor or ends as you lot call it, cause of this postcode bollocks. I mean what's that all about? You ain't in the flipping Bronx. And what makes me laugh; you lot don't even fight one on one, have a straightener. Instead you got ten of you on some poor sod and you're all tooled up as well.'

Tony shook his head half laughing.

'You lot are a bunch of Muppets, if you ask me.'

Malik sat still, searching for a reply but he couldn't find one. Tony's words had pounded into his chest like rock size hailstones. His reputation had got him a long way but he sensed that he was now a small fish sharing a pond with a harbour shark. Tony switched off the engine; he wanted Malik to hear every word he had to say.

'Right ... you see that house?' He pointed to a huge detached property behind a double set of iron gates. A white Range Rover sat proudly on the driveway further demonstrating prosperity. Malik eased his window right down to get a clearer view. He scoped over the mock Tudor style house, adorned with traditional black oak panelling. Two large potted ferns sat either side of an arch that led to the front door and an oversized double garage adjoined the side of the house.

Malik struggled to take in the monstrosity.

'Raaaahhh ... I ain't seen dem type of house Boss. Dat's a few million, right there.'

Tony smirked.

'You like it?'

'Yeah man - pure luxury; I live in a damp little flat, yuh get me.'

Tony produced a grey key fob from his pocket and then pressed a small button on the side. 'Well, guess what?' Instantly the large iron gates slowly glided open. Malik's eyes widened. He didn't know what lesson he was supposed to be learning but he was storing every moment in his memory.

'Oh my days ... is this yuh yard boss?'

'Yeah mate. This is my gaff.'

'Dam, yuh living proper large. I can't believe it.'

Tony swung the Audi roadster onto the driveway and parked up next to the Range Rover.

'Come, follow me.' Tony motioned his head sideways and got out the car.

Malik jumped out.

'Who's duh white Range?'

'Oh that's the wife's, all top spec mate; she loves it.'

Malik looked up at the sheer size of the house. His mind flashed back to his estate and it looked even more dilapidated than before.

Tony turned his keys in the door and pushed it open. He turned to Malik, who was unsure whether to follow him or wait outside.

'Are you just gonna stand there? Come on then.'

Malik followed his boss into the unexpected and was greeted by a sea of white marble floor that flowed into every room. Looking down at his greasy boots he thought it best to remove them.

'Smart move, the missus will chop your nuts off if you get her floor dirty,' Tony jested.

After removing his own boots, he motioned to Malik to follow him down the hallway towards the kitchen. Huge framed oil paintings hung on the walls of the brightly lit space. To the left a winding staircase led upstairs where an extravagant crystal chandelier hung from the ceiling.

'Can I use duh toilet boss?'

'Yeah mate; second door on the left. Meet me in here.'

Tony walked through an arch into a sizeable open plan kitchen with a long centre console down the middle.

Malik hustled down to the toilet, he was busting; this was not helped by the buzz of being inside such a capacious house. As he reached for the door handle, the door swung open and an attractive woman of Asian origin stumbled into his path. She froze on the spot.

'Who are you?'

'Oh sorry, I work for Tony.'

The super petite woman scanned Malik, and then disappeared into the adjacent room.

'Rah, didn't expect dat,' Malik whispered as he relieved himself, trying to match Tony with such a woman and match such a woman with the big Range Rover on the drive.

Confused, Malik headed to the kitchen to join Tony.

'Oh I just met yuh wife, I didn't know she was ...' Malik paused.

Tony swiftly cut in.

'What, tall, gorgeous and fit?'

Malik threw Tony a puzzled glance.

'Tall? She's shorter than me boss, I'm only 5'6.'

'Malik, what are you on about mate? You been smoking that ganja?'

'Tony, is that you?' A voice shouted from the stairwell.

'Bit late if it wasn't me luv, they would have nicked everything by now.'

Malik laughed; he was beginning to see a humorous side to his boss.

'Come down, we got a visitor.'

'I'm here darling.'

Malik span round on the barstool and was dazzled as his eyes settled on the tall Mediterranean woman. Her brown designer hair was immaculate, as were her clothes. Malik never thought that class had a particular smell, until now.

Tony got up, realizing he was being rude.

'Babe, this is my trainee I told you about, Malik. Malik this is my wife Marina.'

Malik jumped down from the stool, transfixed as if Michelle Obama had just walked in.

Marina extended her hand to shake Malik's.

'Hello luv, I've heard a lot about you.'

'Hello.' Malik laughed, slightly embarrassed.

Tony looked at Malik.

'What's wrong with you, you silly sod?'

'I thought dat other lady was yuh wife.'

Marina's eyebrows rose, throwing her husband a poisonous stare. Malik clocked the look and realised he was causing an issue.

'Sorry, I didn't wanna cause nuttin ... I thought the Asian lady ...'

Tony looked at his wife and they both began laughing.

'That's Mai, our cleaner. I can't take you anywhere can I? You'll have me strung up.'

Marina leaned over and gave her husband a kiss on the cheek.

'Going to the hairdresser's darling.'

'What, again? Bloody hell! I might as well let that Nicky Clarke move in; you were only there a couple of days ago.'

Marina ignored him, picked up her Louis Vuitton

handbag and walked out.

Tony turned to Malik.

'Women ... You work hard to make the money and then they work even harder spending it.'

Malik laughed.

Tony walked over to the fridge.

'Wanna beer or something stronger?'

'Nah, a beer's good.'

Tony took out a bottle of Becks and opened it with his teeth before passing it to Malik.

'So Malik ... I hear you're bit of a bad boy.'

'Nah I'm cool man, I just do what I gotta do.'

'You do what you gotta do. What, rob people for a couple of quid or a two bob mobile phone ... sell a bit of weed here and there?'

Malik took a swig of his beer.

'Yeah, I mean, dat's what I do innit ... gotta make my peas.'

'Make your peas.' Tony laughed. 'You make a little pocket change; spend it on a new pair of trainers, then you're bloody skint again.'

Malik hunched his shoulders.

'What else can I do? I got a criminal record. Anyways I didn't really wanna work for nobody, dat's jus long.'

'Look son ... no disrespect, but I drive through your manor now and again. I see you youngsters walking about with your trousers round your kneecaps, I mean you ain't gonna get any respect looking like that. I mean proper respect from people that matter people that can help you go places. It's no good prancing around giving it the large when you ain't got a pot to piss in. Money makes things happen. How many of your friends own a yacht or a nightclub or something on that scale? Probably none, right ... you ain't gotta answer. We all know you ain't going anywhere anytime soon. Look around you ... who has all the money? You gotta get real. I was raised on a tough estate, just like you son. I've been hungry. But my hunger turned into a vision and here I am.

Malik downed some more beer, hoping Dutch courage would rescue him from the Judge Dread who was defacing the picture of his world like an original Picasso painting. Normally he would have knocked Tony out and stomped all over him, but he looked like a man that even a sledgehammer wouldn't put down.

Tony could see the strain in Malik's eyes.

'So you like my gaff?'

'Yeah.' Malik replied, looking around.

Three steps led down from the kitchen to a plush living space. Malik slowly eyed the interior and could see quality oozing from wall to wall. A Victorian style chaise longue in crushed Aubergine velvet sat proudly below an enormous detailed antique mirror, which stood out against the stark white walls. On a grey slate feature wall was a 50 inch flat screen television surrounded by a white L shaped suede sofa.

Malik had only seen such extravagant dwellings, when platinum selling rappers were flossin' their cribs on TV. He gulped down the last of his beer and tried to relax, for the first time in his life he felt vulnerable. At the drop of a hat, his boys would back him in any situation. But now he was alone with the real deal, an old school gangster, who didn't need to say much to scare the crap out of him. But he couldn't show it because if it came to the crunch he would do anything to come out on top.

Tony pointed to a set of smoked glass sliding doors to the right of the living room area.

'Through there, is my gym and 50ft swimming pool.'

Malik gave Tony a knowing glance.

'I can see you hit the weights hard.'

'Yeah, I used to compete mate; won the national championships, back in the 90s ... I'm in my 50s now but I try to keep myself in shape; never know when I might be called upon.'

Malik sat humbly, almost questioning his whereabouts. Briefly, he tried to imagine what his own father would be like but he'd never met him. All he could see was the old photo stuck on the back of his wardrobe door. His mother never spoke about him much and when she did it was always a strain, so he didn't ask about his father that often.

Tony gave him a nudge, breaking his thoughts.

'Anyway, what I'm getting at is, everything I know about cars, I learnt from my old man. I can teach you the trade and you can make yourself a decent living, maybe open your own garage. I'm sure that's what Lenny wants but I'm just gonna keep it real with you. If you wanna take the other path, you gotta go large, but not on my watch, I promised Lenny. In case you haven't noticed, it's not you fellas living in a gaff like this. You're out there fighting over scraps and killing each other for it, while people like me are moving some serious weight. I tell you this because I like you, you're alright-there's something about you, plus a friend of Lenny's is a friend of mine. But let me tell you, unless you're willing to take a set of pliers and snip some poor bastard's fingers off, torture someone close to death or kill someone stone dead, forget about it mate. It's a dark world - you gotta have a big pair of nuts as well as the smarts - because believe me, if you mess up, you'll either do a proper long stretch or they'll be fishing your body out of the Thames ... yuh get me.'

He mocked, but he was deadly serious.

White Powder

Glancing over at the other queues, Aisha watched as a trail of tired travellers ambled through the checkpoint to collect their suitcases. Heathrow was bustling, despite the politicians' rhetoric about a deep recession sweeping the country.

Aisha had only been in the queue for half a minute, but it was half a minute too long. The flight was several hours but felt like days. She just wanted to get back to the familiarity and comfort of her quiet close in Tottenham.

An American family in front exchanged a few words and then were on their way. Aisha stepped up to the desk. A female in her late 40s snatched her passport from her hand.

'Where have you travelled from darling?'

Aisha discretely cut her eye at the officer.

'Miami.'

'Been on holiday?'

Aisha sighed at what she deemed a stupid question.

'Yeah, went to visit my dad, innit.'

'Oh, your dad's American is he?'

'No, he's Jamaican. What's wid the questions?'

'It's just procedure, Miss ... Regan.'

Aisha folded her arms, her defence mechanisms

kicking into auto pilot. She didn't have a lot of patience, especially for people in uniform.

'Look, I don't mean to be rude, yeah, but I got people waiting for me.'

The red haired officer stepped out from her post.

Aisha's eyes followed her.

'Is something wrong?'

'Miss Regan, could you just wait there please.'

Aisha didn't answer.

Just behind the desks, a straight-faced gentleman in a blue polyester uniform was busy eagle eyeing the checkpoints. The officer strolled over and exchanged a few words with him before handing over Aisha's passport, which he held up to the light to scrutinize.

A Nigerian businessman dressed in traditional attire stood at the adjacent desk loudly trying to legitimise his British status. It was enough of a commotion to take Aisha's attention away from her own inconvenience. She didn't need scrutiny, not now. She had to be somewhere.

Dipping in her handbag, Aisha felt around for her mobile phone, remembering that she hadn't picked up any messages. But it was too late for that; the uniformed gentleman rudely invited himself into her personal space, tapping her passport against the palm of his hand,

'Miss Regan?'

Aisha rolled her eyes up into her eyelids.

'Yeah ...'

'I'm the Senior Immigration Officer, could you follow me please.'

'Why, what's wrong?'

The straight-nosed gentleman pompously ignored her.

Aisha fixed her travel bag onto her shoulder and followed the man towards a grey door, guarded by two armed police officers.

After swiping a security card, the man pushed open the door and ushered Aisha into a dimly lit corridor with CCTV cameras peering down from the ceiling. He opened a second door and led Aisha into a small interview room, where there was a table and three chairs. He placed Aisha's documentation down and pulled out a chair for her.

'Take a seat.'

Aisha slumped down in the chair.

'What's happening? Why you brought me in here?'

He sat down, screening Aisha's body language.

'What, you have no idea why you're here?

Aisha threw a scornful glare.

'No I don't, dat's why I'm asking innit.'

The officer picked up the phone and dialled a number, keeping one eye fixed on Aisha.

'Hello, Mary, it's Stephen. Could you come over to the interview suite?' I got a young lady here; I think she's got something to tell us.'

He placed the phone back on the table and

focused on Aisha, who was nervously chewing the last molecules of flavour out of her gum.

The door soon opened and a plus size woman with short spiked hair bowled into the room and pulled out the remaining chair next to her colleague.

'Mary, this is Miss Regan.'

Aisha sat up.

'Can you stop calling me Miss Regan? My name's Aisha, yeah.'

Mary leaned forward, placing her right hand on the desk.

'Ok Miss — Aisha, we just want to ask you a few questions and then you will be on your way. I am here to help you.'

Mary's voice was sympathetic.

Aisha let her shoulders down. Mary had a friendly disposition; a presence that brought some much needed warmth to the empty room.

'Right,' said Stephen. 'Is there anything you might want to tell us?'

'Like what? I just want to go home, yeah. You looked at my passport, ain't nothing wrong with it, but you still got me in here.'

Stephen homed in on Aisha's travel holdall.

'Nice bag. Gucci, is it?'

'Yeah, my dad bought it ... is dat a problem?'

Stephen tapped his index finger annoyingly on the corner of the table in one second intervals.

'Your dad's in Miami, right?'

Aisha frowned.

'Obviously!'

'Close to your dad, are you? I see you visited him once this year already.'

'And so what? If he's paying, then I'm going, innit. What, is it a crime to see my dad now?'

'Well that depends, doesn't it?'

Mary got up and placed a hand on her colleague's shoulder.

'Stephen, can I have a quiet word.'

Stephen threw her a confused glance and then followed her out the room.

Aisha sat fidgeting with her excessively large hoop earrings. She could see the two officers talking to one another through the glass window. Reality began to sink in as she tried to lip read, making up her own mind about what they were discussing.

Mary stood in front of Stephen with hands on her sizeable hips.

'You're being a bit obnoxious, she's only young.'

Stephen peered back through the glass at Aisha.

'She's carrying ... I've had a tip-off. But I want her to come clean.'

'Well, I know she's hiding something. I'm not impressed with her hard nut attitude. She's just scared Stephen ... let me handle it.'

Stephen sighed.

'Ok, ok, you handle it.'

Mary slotted a few coins into the coffee machine

and vended herself a beverage before joining Aisha in the interview room.

She placed her cappuccino on the table and sat back down.

'You're a beautiful young lady, ain't you?'

Aisha felt uncomfortable with the compliment.

'Thank you,'

'You mixed heritage?'

'Yeah, my dad's Jamaican and my mum's Irish.'

'You remind me of that singer, erm, what's her name? Alicia something...'

Aisha smiled. 'Alicia Keys...'

'Yeah, that's the one,'

'Yeah, a lot of people say dat ... I can't sing though.'

Mary laughed.

'I'm sure you can.'

Aisha began to relax the barrier surrounding her and let Mary into her world; a world that was shrinking into a lonely existence.

'So Aisha, is there anything you think you might want to tell me?'

Aisha felt open and gave in to the realisation that her fiery demeanour was not going to save her from the trouble that was deepening in her mind.

'Look, if I own up to stuff, will they go easy on me?'

Mary paused, half pleased with herself.

'I will see what I can do.'

Aisha's lips began to tremble as tears oozed from

her shiny brown eyes.

'I've swallowed twenty condoms of cocaine ... I can't say nothing else. Seriously, I can't.'

Mary handed Aisha a tissue from her shirt pocket.

'You silly girl! What have you got yourself into, aye.'

Aisha wiped away the wetness from her face, smudging her eye makeup.

Mary looked on, saddened.

'Look, you're messing up that pretty face of yours.'

'Am I going prison?'

Mary signalled to her colleague who was still observing from behind the window.

'That will be up to the judge. First we have to retrieve those packages.'

Victor pummelled his finger against the lift button. 'Come on.'

He shuffled back and forth until the lift levelled out on the ground floor. Slipping through the doors before they could fully open, he fired his finger at the car park button, not allowing anyone else a chance to share the ride. He reached into his pocket for his phone and car keys, before quick stepping over to his car. After taking a glance over his shoulder, he disengaged the central locking and eased his slim frame into the X5. Fixing his earpiece, he scrolled through the last calls on his phone and then redialled the last number. He started the car and glided down the winding slope to the exit barrier.

Baron answered after one ring. He'd been pacing up and down his living room for almost two hours waiting for Victor to check in with him.

'Soldier, wha gwaan?'

Victor paused.

'Bredrin, it's bad news ...'

'Victor ... wha yuh ah say?'

'She didn't come through. I asked a woman from the same flight and she said she saw immigration pull her in.'

A loud bang echoed down the phone line. Baron had obviously hit or thrown something in frustration.

'Mi tell yuh dat Aisha gal too feisty, she musa run up her mout ... dat's ah whole heap ah food garn Bredrin.'

'Baron, calm down man.'

'Calm down? Yuh know much money inna dat ... bout calm down,' Baron yelled.

Victor searched for words to calm him. He sensed something wasn't right; they had pulled off numerous runs before without any hitches. Baron had things on lock.

Forty-four year old Barrington Lewis, known as Baron on the street, was a known dangerous individual: a smile-in-your-face-then-kill-you-stone-dead type of man. He'd imported his sadistic reputation over from Jones Town Jamaica and had firmly cemented it across the boroughs of North London. He hated kinks in his normally smooth operation. It meant someone would have to get hurt just so he could make a point. As far as he was concerned, that was standard procedure.

Victor decided to buy himself some time to think as he turned down the slip road on to the M4.

'Look we can't talk about this on the phone, I'm heading to yuh yard.'

Baron kissed his teeth.

'Alright Bredrin, we talk when yuh reach.'

Kia scrambled for her mobile phone, wanting to give whoever was calling the busy tone. Looking down at 'UNKNOWN' flashing on the screen her emotions began to play games with her. Maybe it's Malik, she thought. Or it's that idiot calling me again. She let it ring for a few more seconds and then answered.

'Hello, who is dis?'

A distressed female voice pierced through the receiver.

'Kia it's me; Aisha. They've locked me up, I'm so scared ... I didn't even wanna do it, I—'

'Hold on, slow down. What you talking about? Where are you?'

'I got arrested at Heathrow.'

'Aisha, you're not making any sense. Ain't you in Miami?'

Aisha sniffed down the phone line.

'I came back today, I was carrying stuff and I got caught, innit ... Kia, I'm proper scared.'

Aisha began to sob, worrying Kia.

'Aisha.'

Her friend put the phone back to her ear and took a deep breath.

'Kia, go and see my mum yeah, and tell her I'm sorry, tell her he made me do it ... you know who I'm talking about ... look I got to go, love you.'

Kia held the phone tight to her ears, stunned. She was still trying to absorb her friend's fragmented words.

'Love you too.'

The line went dead. Kia put her head back down on her pillow to support the weight of the burden that had just been thrust upon her. Aisha, her closest friend since reception class, was locked up and deep down a part of her was not surprised. Aisha had changed since getting herself entwined with Ninja. Ninja had huge influence and the credibility she craved. She loved the dangerous mist that kept him fired up. On the flipside, she'd mistakenly identified the showering of designer labels as an act of undying love, forgiving the periodic violence that he often turned on her.

Kia's bedroom door swung open and her mother strolled into the small space.

'Kia, have you got £10 to lend me until I get my

money?'

Kia looked up at her mother in disgust.

'I suppose you want it for weed, yeah?'

'Look, just give me the £10 and stop asking questions.'

'Mum, you're not on the rocks are you? You've been behaving kind of desperate lately.'

'Look, don't bother...forget it.' Angela left the room, slamming shut the bedroom door.

Kia got up and stormed out of her room to confront her mother. Angela was already pulling hard on a half of cigarette she'd found in the ash tray.

'Mum, you really have to sort your life out ... Dad's gone yeah, he was a waste of space. Look how you've just let yourself go.'

Angela didn't respond and stared blankly out of the living room window, still dressed in her stained nightdress. She knew Kia was right and desperately wanted to muster the strength to claw her way out from the depressive hole that had swallowed her and refused to spit her out.

'Mum, I need you to be strong for me, I'm having this baby and I feel alone right now ... Aisha's been locked up, Malik's gone, everything is just coming on top.'

Angela jumped out of her trance-like state.

'What do you mean Aisha's locked up?'

'She just called, I think she's at the airport, I'm not sure.'

'What are you saying Kia?'

'She's been caught carrying drugs, Mum.'

Angela held her head and looked up at the ceiling.

'Oh Lord ... how did she end up in that mix up?'

'It's probably something to do with Ninja.'

Angela looked at her daughter, clearly puzzled.

'Who's Ninja?'

'Nathan Lewis Mum, remember he used to go to my school before he got sent to that Pupil Referral Unit.

'Oh him, that bad breed ... what's she doing with that ugly cruft?'

'Boy's got money, innit. Ain't you noticed all her designer clothes when she comes round here, she ain't working.'

Something was resonating in Angela's mind. For the first time in a long time she felt ashamed of her sorry state. She grabbed a faded towel that was draped over the radiator.

'I'm going to have a shower; we have to go and see her mum.'

Kia looked oddly at her. 'Are you serious?'

'Yes I'm serious. We'll give this flat a good clean and then we'll drive up there.'

Angela moved towards Kia with outstretched arms.

'Come here.'

Kia turned back towards her bedroom.

'I'm not ready for that Mum.'

The Plan

With his head still buried in the pillow Malik waited for Tony to answer the phone. After several rings a female voice filtered through the line. 'Ace Audi, can I help you?'

'Zoe, it's Malik, where's Tony?'

'He's gone to pick up a car with Gary. How comes you're not in work?'

Malik sniffed.

'I got the flu, Zoe.'

'Aww, you poor darling…got man flu'

'Nah, don't take duh Mick. I'm proper shivering and everything.'

'Oh, ok I'll tell Tony when he comes back. You take care, hun.'

She didn't believe him, but let it slide.

Malik slipped the phone back under the pillow; he was two months into his apprenticeship and attending college, studying the theory of motor mechanics. He'd made himself a stranger to the night and the cold streets where he used to prey on easy targets. Ninja was still in prison but was unusually quiet. The quiet was worse than an oncoming storm; the paranoia had Malik wary of every shape and shadow that came too close. He wanted to get away from the seemingly forgotten estate that was so far removed from the minds of the ruling class.

Malik reached into the top drawer of his battered bedside cabinet and removed a crumpled sheet of paper and pencil. Although he enjoyed working with Tony, it was painfully long and the money wasn't coming quick enough. He had hardly chipped away a rock from his mother's mountain of bills. He looked up at the damp patch that had settled in the corner of the ceiling and bent his face out of shape with disgust.

He began studying his notes, memorising the route that he carefully mapped out. Pleased with his jottings, he picked up his lighter and lit the corner of the paper, placing it in the ash tray. He then took a cigarette out from a half empty packet and then opened the bedroom window before perching himself on the window ledge.

As he blew out the smoke, he felt a whirl of optimism stirring in his stomach. He was sure that he could pull off the move; it was easy pickings as far as he was concerned. The potential earnings far outweighed the risk of getting caught. With Tony firm in his mind it was easy to put the vision of

prison into the most secluded part of his mind. I gotta go large, he thought.

Down below, a hooded youth idly cycled passed on a rusty BMX openly advertising the freshly built spliff that was dangling from the corner of his mouth. Malik instantly knew that the very animated movement and the large body mass belonged to Tubbs. He quickly opened the window wider to get his attention.

'Yo, Tubbs! Up here fam.'

The youth stopped the bike and looked up towards Malik's second floor flat.

'Wha gwaan, Murkz. Ain't seen you for time ... you've been missing.'

'Yeah I know ... listen, bring that ting and come.'

Tubbs held up the spliff and grinned.

Malik grinned back.

'Yeah, dat.'

His friend dismounted the bike and headed towards the communal door. Malik quickly pulled a pair of track bottoms over his boxers and sprayed some Lynx over his unwashed body, conscious of his morning odour. Once inside, Tubbs lowered his large frame down onto a fold up chair in the corner of the room.

'Tubbs, mind you don't bruk my chair.'

Tubbs lit the spliff.

'Shut up man.'

'Nah, seriously. You've put on some size since school days, you must be eating pure Big Mac and ting.'

Tubbs blew out the smoke and then quickly interjected into Malik's flow, avoiding the ridicule.

'Anyway, what's happening? You ain't been on road for time.'

Malik paused, feeling slightly weak about the fact he'd been keeping a low profile.

'I got an apprenticeship innit, trying to do tings differently, yuh get me.'

Tubbs nodded in agreement, but was unconvinced, studying his friend as he passed over the spliff. Tubbs knew Malik well. Since coming over from Nigeria at the age of eight Malik had backed him and dealt with a lot of altercations on his behalf. Tubbs looked up to Malik; he loved his many personalities and the respect he commanded on the street. It was unusual not to see his friend out in the midst of the dramas that filtered through the decaying estates.

Tubbs soon broke the cloud of silence that had ascended into the room.

'It's Ninja innit?'

Malik tilted his head back and blew the smoke up towards the ceiling.

'Tubbs, you know me yeah, I ain't afraid of nobody ... but Ninja. Ninja is off key, he's evil blud! ... I know he's plotting something, I feel it.'

Tubbs went quiet; his plump face smothered with concern.

Malik felt uncomfortable showing a weakness in his usually solid armour, but this was Ninja; sadistic and bordering on crazy. He began rubbing his hands together.

'Anyway Tubbs, bun dat for now. We got bigger

tings to discuss.'

Tubbs finished smoking and stubbed the end out in the ashtray, noticing the fragments of Malik's plans.

'What's dis paper in the ashtray, love letter to Kia? Yuh gone soft, Murkz.'

'What yuh talking about? Me and her done! Dat paper's duh plans blud. Have to destroy the evidence like proper gangster, yuh get me!'

Tubbs sat up and leaned forward in the chair.

'What yuh saying Murkz?'

Malik caressed his goatee, wondering whether to share the details or wait for his other associates to arrive.

'I planned a proper move when I was inside. I mean a big money ting, not no teefing man's oyster card. I'm talking Rolexes, diamond rings. My cousins over south sides have done it a couple times, standard. Dem man are rolling in top of the range BMs, Mercs, everyting'.

Tubbs removed his cap and hoodie to reveal a thirsty grin that was dripping with anticipation.

'What yuh waiting for? Tell me den.'

'Waiting for Tempo and Stuart to reach, I called dem man last night.'

'How come yuh never called me then?'

'I tried your phone nuff times; you must have been face down in yuh Jollof rice, that's why you never hear nuttin.'

'Yeah funny, you're taking liberties. Who is Stuart anyway? Why are you bringing in outside man?'

'Just wait Tubbs, I'll explain later.'

The intercom buzzer started wailing.

'Dat's dem lot ... let dem in Tubbs.'

Malik switched on his laptop and waited for the others to return. He was fired up and knew his boys were just as hungry as he was. They wanted to taste some premium cake and were tired of the economy sponge that the government was leaving them to fight over. Tubbs re-entered the room, followed by Tempo and Stuart.

Tempo, in his usual hyper manner, punched Malik in the chest and sat on the bed.

'Yes Murkz, yuh good?'

'Yeah, man'z good still ... wha gwaan?'

Tempo touched fist with Malik.

'Everyting's cool man.'

Tubbs parked himself back in the chair, leaving Stuart standing in the doorway.

'Stuart, why yuh standing up there all quiet? Come, sit down man.'

Malik motioned with his head, before moving his laptop to make room.

Stuart sat down and held his hand out to shake Malik's.

'Alright mate.'

His strong Irish tone got Tubbs' attention.

'Are you Welsh, fam?'

'You fool.' Malik laughed. 'My man's Irish.'

Stuart was the youngest but looked the oldest in the group, at just 17 he had already served three years in a young offender's institution for armed robbery. Malik had met him on the mechanics course and soon realised that although they came from different backgrounds their lives bore many similarities.

Stuart was quiet and unassuming; in his designer glasses and spiked hair he would appear to be quite studious to those who didn't know him. Tempo on the other hand was full of himself, tall, dark, rather skinny and annoyingly over confident, a confidence that had Malik second guessing whether to include him. Tubbs drew the chair up towards the bed to huddle around the laptop. After loading the website, Malik positioned the screen for all to see.

'There it is boys', that's our ticket right there.' Displayed on the screen was an exclusive looking jewellery shop with large chrome lettering: Dimez of Sloane St.

Tubbs was first to speak.

'Rah, are we gonna rob it?'

Tempo flicked Tubbs in the back of his head.

'Nah Tubbs, we're going to knock on the door and say, "Please Sir, can we have some diamonds?" Of course we're gonna rob it, yuh wasteman!'

Tubbs went quiet and Malik's stare told him everything he needed to know.

'Right, here's the plan. Stuart, get yourself a crisp suit and I want you to visit the shop a couple times, blag it about how you wanna buy something nice for duh wifey, but you can't make up your mind. Gain their trust…, yuh get me. Tell dem you're one a dem city traders or suttin. While yuh in there, clock the cabinets, security cameras … anyting you can find out.'

Stuart nodded.

'Yeah, I got it.'

Malik continued.

'I got to check one yout called Sticky. I hear he's the man to get us some mopeds … and den I'm going to borrow some club hammers from my garage.'

Tempo cracked his knuckles.

'Sounds good still.'

Malik grinned.

'Yeah man, got dis ting planned, nuttin long, just in and out. Stuart, hear what: on the day you're gonna be the man to get them to open the door. Yuh done know they got some intercom and shit, they ain't letting no black youts up in their shop, trust me.'

Stuart stayed silent, slowly nodding in agreement.

'We gotta time this ting perfect. We buss round the corner just as Stuart is gaining entry' Malik paused. 'Sorry Stuart, but we're gonna have to fling you down on the floor and rough you up a bit, style it out and dat.'

Malik placed his hand on Tubbs's shoulder.

'Tubbs, you threaten the staff wid yuh big self, while me and Tempo smash the glass and bag up the jewels.'

Malik looked at his three friends, one by one, his face deadly serious.

'Sixty seconds in and out.'

They all touched fists.

Tempo began rubbing his hands with excitement.

'Gonna buy a bad boy car.'

This upset Malik.

'Tempo, don't get all excited and bait us up, you need to just humble on this one yeah.'

Malik wasn't to be crossed and he knew it.

Tempo held his tongue and changed the subject.

'Alright, who's got da Rizla, cos I got weed.'

He chuckled as he sniffed the fresh bag which he removed from inside his sock.

Malik plugged the speaker cable into the laptop and then scrolled through his music library for a tune appropriate for the moment. Stuart passed a pack of cigarette papers to Tempo, who began methodically constructing a masterpiece.

A heavy grime tune began reverberating from the walls, filling the room with a manic bassline that instantly had them bobbing their heads in unison

Behind the Walls of Scotland Yard

David folded the newspaper and dismissively shoved it to one side.

'Bloody Olympics! We didn't even ask for it, and we still had to pay for it. I mean they don't even do much sport in school nowadays. So, how was it for the younger generation? Lying sods.'

His wife, Margaret, strolled into kitchen.

'Moaning again, luv?'

'I'm not moaning, I'm just saying it as I see it. I've been in the force for 30 years now and I've seen the changes. These kids don't care for nothing, I mean look at the riots last year.'

He took a swig of coffee.

'I thought I was watching *Planet of the Apes*, the way they were looting those shops ... and then they wanna blame us, thieving little bastards.'

Margaret strolled over to the breakfast table and began fixing her husband's tie.

'Now that's why I fell in love with you, you have such a way with words.'

Fifty-year old David Wilkes was in love with the police force, he had worked through the ranks up to Detective Chief Inspector for the CID. His closest colleagues had aptly named him 'Sherlock' for his investigating tenacity, but recent Government cutbacks and pointless bureaucracy was taking its toll. Loyalty to the establishment was becoming a tall order to maintain, nevertheless, he kept his cards close to his chest, even away from his trusting wife.

It was 5am and the chill from outside was creeping in through the broken draft excluder under the front door. David got up from the table and put his coat over his burly frame, before picking up his car keys. He ran his hand back through his silver hair, before turning to his wife.

'Right ... back to the jungle.'

Margaret looked up from the ironing board as she took another white shirt from the pile.

'Time's flying, you'll retire soon. It will come before you know it.'

David fumbled with his buttons; he appeared to be uncomfortable with his wife's statement.

'It'll come sooner than you think, luv.'

He spoke under his breath but a part of him wanted her to hear.

She did hear and had stopped ironing.

'What do you mean by that?'

He dismissed her and headed for the front door.

'I see you later darling.'

Outside the semi-detached house, a new Jaguar XJ sat proudly on the driveway. Although covered in a thin sheet of morning frost its beauty still showed under the glow of the moonlight. David cast an admiring look over his new motor before opening the door and getting inside.

Looking in the rear view mirror, his reflection spoke to him.

'She has no idea of what I've become.'

He started the engine with a touch of guilt but it soon disappeared under a cloud of self-importance.

'Right, settle down lads. I'm Detective Superintendent Rogers — Mark Rogers — and this is DCI David Wilkes.'

David gave a nod of acknowledgement.

'Good morning lads.'

'Good morning Guv,' flooded back from the room.

A sea of bulletproof vests, sat regimentally behind three rows of desks, talking among themselves. They were alert and fully charged, even though the birds had barely finished singing the morning blues. The men and one woman were mainly from the Hampshire Police force, except for two seasoned London detectives, Matthews and Thompson.

Rogers adjusted the projector and double-clicked the mouse on the laptop.

'Attention lads ... and you Karen.'

He gave the only female officer an acknowledging smile.

'Welcome to *Operation Pebble*. Now, this is Roman Ferguson.'

He pointed to a slightly distorted image of a built light-skinned youth.

'He has become quite a big fish in that dirty little pond they call the Howberry Estate. We're pretty sure that he is responsible for distributing crack cocaine, at least one rape and whispers on the ground tell us that he is, more than likely behind the murder of that young footballer Odoku. Word has it that Odoku refused to conceal some weapons for Ferguson, so he put a contract out on him ... well, probably paid some stupid kid 50 quid to bump him off.'

Thompson coughed, trying to contain his amusement.

'That's bloody ridiculous; these black kids are off their heads.'

Rogers glanced over in his direction.

'Thompson, we got to be political correct now, you know the drill.'

'Sorry boss! Just, still can't get my head round it.'

Rogers went on to the next slide.

'We've had a tip off about a crack house being run from this disused garage which is situated directly at the back of the flats, backing on to the houses on Fenbury Street. Now we've had surveillance running on the estate for about three months and have identified some of the runners, although it's proving difficult to identify who is who because they're always hooded up. But, one thing they do have in common is the purple bandanas. Now, Roman Ferguson is currently out on license but we haven't been able to pin him down for anything serious.

Nobody wants to talk, we got more chance of getting a politician to speak the truth.

Rogers motioned his hand towards David, who stepped forward to take over.

'Gentleman ... modern technology is a beautiful thing because now we have something called 'You Tube'. It tells us a lovely story about some gang members on the streets of London. I mean we don't even have to ask their names anymore, because if you listen to their songs carefully enough, they tell us for free, it's wonderful. So back to the purple bandanas. From our investigations we have established that they belong to a gang called the 'Milly Boys'.'

A roar of laughter filled the room. Wilkes clapped his hands together. 'Gentleman, please...this is no laughing matter. The media are jumping all over this so-called 'Black-on-Black' crime, so we've got to start getting some results and take down some of the main players. Now the name 'Milly', if you haven't worked it out already, is derived from 9mm. Stupid name, I know, but we have to take them seriously. We've had two shootings in Hackney, one in Tottenham and, more recently, a stabbing in Stoke Newington. These have all occurred in the last six weeks.'

David clicked on the next slide.

'Now here we have some potential suspects ... the youngest, probably 13 or so and the oldest roughly 17 or 18. If you look closely—'

The Inspector zoomed in on the image of the

huddled group, who were proudly performing gang gestures, but it soon became apparent what he was drawing the men's attention to.

'Now this boy is clearly only about 13 years old and he is blatantly brandishing a Mac 10 semi-automatic in broad daylight. Now for some of you Hampshire lot, this is a far cry from nicking people for stealing sheep. This is London. These kids are a different breed.'

Rogers stepped forward.

'On your tables is a full brief of today's operation. We got to seem to be doing something and if we get that Mac 10 off the street, that will be a bonus. Now any questions?'

'No Sir,' echoed in reply.

Rogers was no nonsense, hard and extremely patriotic. Having served in the Gulf War and as a Detective Inspector on the streets of Manchester, he had recently transferred to London to help with the spiralling crime figures. Gangs were his forte; he'd seen it all — ride-by shootings, 10-year-old drug dealers - He'd witnessed it and dealt with it all first hand.

Rogers checked his wristwatch and then closed the briefing. 'Right, it is 6.15am; I want you on site and hitting them doors by 6.45am. Good luck, lads.'

DCI Wilkes slowly eased the silver Jaguar over the speed bumps and then turned left between a set of red units on a large derelict industrial estate. He surveyed the open space, before stopping the car and switching off the engine.

Rogers laughed from the passenger seat.

'Car runs beautifully, Detective... all the sweeter, knowing it was bought with ill-gotten gains.'

David smiled, satisfied with his purchase.

'Yes it does feel good, I must agree. Anyway, what brings us out here?'

Rogers ran his hand back through his mousey hair, indicating that something was wrong or he was about to say something that David didn't want to hear.

'I have been doing a lot of homework Dave, putting things into position. I mean if all goes well, this time next year we'll be on a yacht, basking on a Rio beach, drinking cocktails.'

Wilkes looked over at Rogers through half closed eyes.

'Well, do you wanna fill me in?'

Rogers checked the coast for prying eyes. A homeless man ambled past with a shopping trolley full of his life's possessions. He stopped, let out some obscenities and disappeared into a disused unit.

Roger's made a second check and turned back to his colleague.

'You know that journalist in that robbery mix up,

Katherine what's-her-name —'

Wilkes cut in.

'Katherine Peterson.'

Yeah, that's the bird. Anyway, she's been sniffing around for a story. She wants inside information on Baron's criminal history, and also the first bite when we take Baron down. I mean let's face it Baron is a major player as far as organised crime goes.'

Wilkes's face turned from intrigue to puzzlement.

'What are you talking about? And where did you meet her anyway?'

'I met her in that bar over Tower Bridge, you know the one on the corner of Tooley Street. We got talking about stuff, mainly politics, the economy - boring stuff really. Then she starts going on about the black kids that robbed her. You know what women are like after a few drinks ... they start getting all emotional.'

'So let me guess, you decided to take advantage,' Wilkes interrupted.

Rogers smirked mischievously.

'Well, let's say I saw an opportunity ... I made her an offer. I asked her if there was any way she could say that she made a mistake when she picked Simms out from the ID parade and maybe it was Nathan Lewis ... You know-Baron's son. It's not like he's not a nasty little criminal anyway. Then I promised her all the info on Baron and I said I'd give her the whole thing when we take him down. She's desperate, mate. She'll do anything for a decent story.'

'Hold on … you're losing me. Why would you wanna do that?'

'I just wanted to send out a message, to let Baron know that we can do anything, at any given moment. He loves his boy, so you know what I'm getting at.'

'No, I'm not sure I do … I don't like the sound of this.'

'Look, I had his drugs mule picked up at Heathrow; he's got no idea how many informants I've got on the street. Then I had his son shafted, courtesy of Katherine. Since then he's been calling me, asking for all sorts of favours. So I got him to agree to a 30% cut for the return of his son and his drugs.'

Wilkes angrily slammed his hand down on the dashboard.

'Rogers, have you lost your mind? I thought we were going to make a bit of money and then pull the plug. You're not flipping Al Capone, you're DSI Rogers. Have you forgotten?'

Rogers turned his hands upwards.

'Look Dave, the Government is shafting us and they know full well we can't bloody strike. So right now I have had enough of being squeaky clean. The politicians are all bent, so we might as well join them and make some serious money. They're not going to suspect two high ranked officers are they?

David put his right hand to his chin, steadying his head which was filling up with a crowd of possibilities.

'Who else knows about this?'

'Thompson and Matthews. They're doing a lot of work on the ground for us.'

'So how are you going to get Baron's son out?'

'That's easy ... Peterson is going to drop the charges. Claim she was confused, traumatic stress and all that jargon.'

'Oh, I see. And it's all going to be worth it, is it?'

Rogers gave David a meaningful look.

'Trust me on this one, it's all under control. I've got Baron, *right* where we want him.'

Wilkes worryingly twitched his head from side to side.

'Trust you? This is getting way too serious. The wife doesn't have a clue. I almost told the poor cow this morning.'

Rogers opened the window to let in some air.

'Look, we can pull it off Dave, just be the best detective you can be in the meantime. We can't give anybody as much as a sniff at what we're doing.'

'Okay, and what about the original robber?'

'Oh, he's gone off the radar. Officers on the ground say he seems to be going straight. We thought he might have been one of the drug runners, but turns out he knows the 'Milly Boy's' but he's not affiliated.'

'Well don't you think Baron's son will retaliate? As far as he's concerned, he was unfairly locked up, so he's probably going to blame the other chap ...

What's his name?'

'The other kid ... Simms, Malik Simms.'

'Yeah, that's the fella. Has he got form?'

'Yeah, mainly street robbery, possession of cannabis and an ABH charge ... knocked some bloke out with one punch.'

Wilkes put his head back and chuckled for the first time, lightening the mood.

'What was that all about?'

'Oh, that Simms was in a chicken shop on Hackney Road and some Polish bloke jumped the queue, so he wasn't having it and got into an argument with him. Then the Polish fella only went and called him the 'N' word. Bang! That Simms knocked him out cold.'

Wilkes shook his head, amused at the story.

'How do you know all this?'

'Good mate of mine is a constable in Hackney. He's the one who looked at the CCTV and arrested Simms ... apparently it was some punch.'

Wilkes was thinking he'd put his career hat back on after getting so engrossed in the corrupt curriculum.

'Look, I think we need to put some extra officers on the ground, just to form a police presence. It's highly likely that there will be some casualties, especially if Baron's son Nathan gets released. I'm surprised that anything hasn't occurred already.'

'Yeah I agree. I'll get on to it right away.'

Rogers' mobile began ringing.

'Hello, Rogers speaking.'

'Guv, it's Thompson. We've got six members of the Milly Boys in custody, but no sign of Ferguson.'

'Good work, debriefing at 3pm. I'll see you then. Oh, Thompson, did you get anything?'

'Bit of marijuana, a converted pistol and a few dodgy looking knives. Dat's about it Guv.'

'Ok, see you at the yard.'

Rogers placed his phone on the dashboard.

D.O.A

Outside was cold and uninviting to the many summer dwellers that had gone into hibernation, leaving the estate and the surrounding pavements desolate — apart from the swaying silhouettes of a few hard-core alcoholics who were happily drowning in economy cider. Police sirens reverberated from the nearby High Street buildings, then gradually filtered out into the distance. Lenny sat down, not even acknowledging the loud wailing; the sound was just as familiar to him as the beeping from the pedestrian crossing outside his front window.

He removed his glasses and began buffing off the smears with his t-shirt as he turned his head towards the kitchen.

'How was court today babe?'

Marcia appeared in the doorway, still dressed in a grey pencil skirt and matching blazer. She had just arrived home after finishing off some casework at the office.

'I've had a long day, darling. You wouldn't believe I'm representing a 13 year old on a murder charge.'

'Thirteen!' Lenny repeated, alarmed.

'Exactly. In all my years studying law it never even crossed my mind that I would be representing child murderers. I mean, what were *we* doing at thirteen?'

Lenny put his glasses back on .

'Thirteen? I was riding my bike, playing *'knock down ginger'* or something...'

Marcia sighed.

'So how did we get from that to stabbing each other like it's a new hobby or something?'

'I know babe, I'm around these kids every day. And one thing I've noticed is that most of them ain't got a dad in their life. Did you know that roughly 49% of black youths are being raised in a single parent household? I mean some men are quick to dig in the soil to plant the seed, but then not as quick to help out with the gardening. If you see a plant withering with damaged leaves, that's an obvious sign that it hasn't been correctly nurtured. That's just how nature works and kids ain't any different

'Don't get me wrong, I know a lot a women do a good job, but I still think a man's role is vital. And I mean a proper man, not one of them trainer buyer man. You know, the man that turns up every six months and buys the *yout* a pair of trainers and then vanishes. Now that's just ridiculous! You got kids out there thinking their dad is some kind of Foot Locker Fairy.'

Marcia laughed.

'Yeah, so true ... but to be honest, a lot of us adults are damaged too. I suppose it's about breaking the cycle. Well, at least Malik is off this roadman thing now ... isn't he?'

Lenny looked up, unsure.

'Well yeah, but Tony called me the other day ... said that Malik's been acting strange, like his mind is not on the job.'

'Oh. Have you called him?'

'Nah, I've been busy ... but I'm gonna call him later, he's been on my mind.'

Marcia studied her husband for few seconds, then walked over to the sofa and threw her arms around his shoulders.

'I love you so much.'

Lenny looked up admiringly. She was still as beautiful as when he first met her and hadn't changed much in the 12 years. Looking at her flawless dark features, he raised his hand and began twisting the end of one her neat dreadlocks.

'What's that for?'

Marcia gazed back at him.

'I am just so proud of you. You were just like these boys when I met you and you were what, 28? You could have died out there, the rate you were going.'

Lenny went quiet, thinking back. 'Yeah ... mad times.'

Marcia softly massaged his neck.

'Look at you now ... These boys look up to you.'

Despite her reflections, Lenny could see sadness in his wife's eyes.

'Are you ok?'

'I'm sorry; it's just been a really emotional day. It's just frightening to see how lost some of these boys are.'

'It's ok; I know where you're at.'

Marcia sat down and picked up the remote.

'If you see how this little 13 year old boy had all his little gang friends up in the court, like it was some tea party.'

Lenny put his arm around Marcia's shoulder and pulled her close.

'I know it's difficult for you, but you have to try and keep your emotions separate from your cases, otherwise things can get distorted.'

'I know hun. Let me get the dinner and we can watch a film.'

'Yeah that sounds good ... but I have to call Malik at some stage.'

Malik stood at the window mulling over the robbery again and again, psychologically making it a reality and the right thing to do. Sticky was due to drop off a moped at 9pm, the sledge hammers were already tucked under the bed, along with the gloves and some extravagant ski masks. He was ready to go out on a limb; a limb he hoped wouldn't break and drop him right back in a jail cell. 'Malik.'

He jumped from his thoughts. He hadn't even noticed his mother sitting on the sofa.

'Yeah Mum.'

'You're miles away. What are you studying so hard?'

'Nuttin- I'm just thinking about what I wanna do with my life.'

Jennifer sipped her coffee. She was tired after having completed her shift in the housing department, and had a couple of hours to spare before she left for her cleaning job at the betting shop.

'Come sit down, son.'

'Ah Mum, not another lecture, please.'

Malik reluctantly dragged his feet across the living room and sat down next to his mother.

'We haven't touched base in a while. We're like two strangers living under the same roof. I'm working, studying; you're doing your mechanic thing ...'

'Yeah Mum, it has been a while still.'

Jennifer placed her free hand his shoulder.

'We don't get time to talk, son.'

'Yeah I know Mum, that's how they've got us innit ... on some slave ting.'

'Yes, but what else can we do? I have to keep the roof over our head.'

'But look where we're living Mum. The flat's got mice, damp and what's the council doing about it? Nuttin, cos they don't business.'

'Look, all I can say is I am going to finish my

degree, as hard as it is. I am going to finish. Then I'll have more options to earn more money.'

'But dat's long Mum. I'm tired of round 'ere. I wanna live in a nice house. You should see my boss' yard: electric gates and everyting. His wife is pushing a big Range Rover and they got a maid. I'm like '*Rah*' dis is proper.'

'You shouldn't watch other people. I'm sure your boss had a completely different life from yours.'

'Nah Mum, it wasn't dat much different. He just done tings differently, yuh get me.'

Jennifer threw him a searching look.

'No, I'm not sure I do get you.'

Malik cunningly dodged his mother's glare and changed the direction of the conversation.

'You look tired Mum, you need some pampering.'

'I can't afford luxuries Malik, you know that.'

'Nah Mum, you've lost that sparkle from yuh face. Man used to queue up to take you out.'

'What you saying, I'm not attractive anymore?'

'You are, but ... you know what I'm trying to say.'

Jennifer got up.

'Where are you going, Mum?'

She didn't answer, and strolled into her bedroom, closing the door behind her.

Malik buried his head into his hands.

'Damn! I messed up.'

Jennifer edged over to the mirror which was

attached to an old dressing table that her mother had given her. She leaned over, apprehensive of who would be staring back at her. Look at me, she thought, as her reflexion appeared in the glass. All that her son painstakingly tried to say without offending her was now being confirmed. Beneath her hazel eyes were the shadows of sleep deprivation. Her silky caramel skin looked blotchy; mainly due to a smash and grab diet. She looked up to the ceiling.

'Lord, give me strength.' She whispered, confident that God had heard her.

Malik checked the time. It was 9.20pm, Sticky was late. A surge of anxiety began to bring discomfort to his stomach, but he was unsure whether it was because he'd upset his mother or the imminent arrival of the moped. He wondered what had happened to his own moped, which was stolen from the communal car park.

A text message lit up on his cracked phone screen: *Soon come. Sticky.*

Malik slipped into his bedroom for his puffa jacket, ready to meet the cold. He ran his eyes under the bed to make sure the tools hadn't magically vanished. Everything was there. It all felt real, his plan was coming alive.

The doorbell rang. Malik didn't respond, almost as if he hadn't heard it.

'Malik,' Jennifer shouted from behind her bedroom door.

'Who's at the door?'

'A Bredrin Mum. I was supposed to meet him downstairs, don't know why he's ringing off the doorbell.' He made his way to the door. 'Sticky, I'm coming, hold on.'

Malik released the security chain, opened the door and was greeted by an unknown tall youth, dressed in all black.

Malik screwed him down.

'You ain't Sticky.'

'Do I look like Sticky? Yuh slipping, blud!'

Realising the imminent danger, Malik turned his head back into the flat.

'Mum!! Stay in yuh room,' he shouted, hoping his mother had heard him.

A foot smashed into the front door, sending him and the door backwards.

'Come we done him,' another voice filtered from behind the front man.

Malik regained balance and backed himself out of the confined passageway towards the living room.

'Maliiiiik!!'

Jennifer screamed from behind her bedroom door as the sound of multiple feet rumbled down the hallway.

The tall youth was first to enter the living room. Adrenaline rushed through Malik's body as the youth was on him in seconds. His eyes glazed out from a green bandana which was covering his face.

Malik side-stepped and then smashed a right hook into his chin, sending him sideways across the glass coffee table which shattered under the impact.

Amidst the breaking glass, Jennifer's screams pierced through Malik's head as three more youths entered the room. A dark stocky boy sprang forward, his hand buried inside his jacket.

'Klash, shank him blud. Show him how we roll, man,' another voice spat from behind, enraging the youth who then pulled the concealed knife.

Malik snapped.

'Come on, blud!!!'

The youth tugged the bandana away from his face.

'Wot you ah bad man Murkz?'

Malik didn't wait a second, grabbing a dining chair and swinging it as the youth lunged in. A violent snap, entwined with a just as violent scream echoed across the room as the chair broke across the youth's head, putting him straight down.

Still holding the broken chair, Malik's mind went into frenzy with thoughts of Kia and his unborn child. His own funeral, his mother crying, vividly came to him all at once. He suddenly remembered the knife, but before he could scan for it the remaining two youths were on him.

The tall youth rose up from the broken coffee table, picking up a large shard of glass from the carnage. He moved to join his two friends, who were now trading punches with Malik. He tossed back his head and laughed towards the ceiling.

'Murkz! Yuh gonna dead, blud!'

Jennifer frantically paced the room, her phone glued to her face.

'Metropolitan Police, how can I help?'

'Hello, they're attacking my son ... you need to come quick!'

'Slow down madam, who's attacking your son.'

'Some boys ... they're in my house! I don't know how many ... just hurry up please!'

'Are they armed?'

'For God sake, I don't know.'

'Ok, what's the address madam?'

'Erm ... 15 Shelton House, Howberry Estate E8...' She held the phone up in the air hoping that the operator would hear the audible mayhem coming from the adjacent room.

'Listen, can you hear?'

'A unit is on its way madam.'

'Ok thank you.'

Jennifer hung up and looked up to the ceiling. 'God please, no.'

The sound of heavy footsteps echoed through the passageway and then all went quiet. She slowly cracked open the door.

'Malik?'

'I'm in here, Mum ... they've gone.'

Jennifer ran into the living room, stumbling into the aftermath. She froze instinctively as her worst fears hit her all at once.

'Oh my God,' she croaked, her voice trembling.

Broken furniture and fragments of glass were strewn across the room. The walls were peppered with fresh blood which at first looked unrealistic, like a staged crime scene. She turned to Malik, who was now struggling up from beneath the upturned dining table.

'They ain't killing me mum. I dealt wid dem.'

Jennifer put her hand to her mouth.

'Oh my God, Malik! They've stabbed you.'

Malik looked down to his midriff.

'Oh shit...'

Just above the right side of his waist, dark blood was now soaking into his t-shirt.

On the floor among the glass, Malik's mobile began ringing. Jennifer grabbed for it, seeing Lenny's name flashing on the screen.

'Lenny, Lenny! They've stabbed Malik.'

'What?! Who?'

'Some boys' ran up in my house.'

'Alright, I'm coming, have you called an ambulance?'

'Oh God, no I haven't ... Hurry up Len, please just come.'

Malik began to slump.

'Mum...'

Jennifer ran to the bathroom and dragged a towel off the radiator, while dialling for an ambulance with her free hand. She soon returned to the room. Malik was now lying on the floor holding his side, groaning under his breath.

'Mum, I'm not dying today, you hear me.'

Jennifer crouched down next to her son, bunched one corner of the sheet and pressed it against the wound. Wedging the phone between her cheek and her shoulder, she stroked his face with her other hand.

'Not today Baby.'

Lenny muted the television and sprang up from the sofa.

'Malik's been stabbed'

Marcia's face widened.

'Oh my God!'

Lenny threw the TV remote across the room; the news instantly stirred up the suppressed anger inside him. Of all the teenagers he worked with, he had a real admiration for Malik. He was his golden boy, the special one.

He desperately tried gathering his thoughts; a heavy weight descended on his chest, entwined with a tinge of guilt.

'I knew something was not right ... all day he's been on my mind.'

Marcia held her husband's hand.

'So was that Jennifer?'

'Yeah, I don't think she'd even called the ambulance ... she must be going out of her mind.'

Marcia looked vacantly at the ground.

'That poor woman.'

Lenny grabbed his coat and car keys.

'Right, I need to get myself down the hospital. I'll see you later.'

Marcia jumped up and stopped him at the door. She removed his glasses and looked deep into his eyes. 'Be strong for them, they need you.' She kissed him softly.

Lenny sighed. 'I will. See you later.'

A light drizzle began to sprinkle the pavement as Lenny exited the front gate. He took out his phone and scrolled for Jennifer's number as he opened his car door. The phone rang before he could press the call button, it was Jennifer.

'Jennifer, I was just going to ring you. How is he?'

'I'm not sure Len. He's lost quite a bit of blood, but he's conscious. We've just got to the hospital.'

'Jennifer, listen to me.'

'I'm listening Len.' Her voice began to crack. 'I can't lose my boy.'

'Stay positive ... We're not losing him, yuh hear me?'

'Ok. Are you on your way?'

'Yeah, I'm in the car, be there in 10 minutes.'

'Thank you Lenny.'

'Alright, soon come.'

Lenny stepped on the accelerator to beat the red light and then turned onto the high road.

'Miss Simms?'

Jennifer eased herself up from the bench.

'Yes.'

The Asian doctor extended his hand and greeted her with a pleasant smile.

'I'm Doctor Hassan, I've been tending to your son this evening.'

Jennifer held her hands together as if she was about to pray.

'Please tell me he's okay.'

The doctor placed a comforting hand on her shoulder, sending a cold chill through her body.

'Your son is going to be ok Madam... '

Jennifer heaved, then exhaled.

'Oh thank God.'

'The wound was mainly superficial, just through the flesh on his waistline. The knife missed any major artery. We've managed to stem the bleeding and the nurse is stitching him up now.'

'Jennifer,' a voice called from across the hallway.

Jennifer turned to see Lenny stepping out from the lift.

The doctor acknowledged him.

'His father?'

Jennifer smiled.

'Oh no, his mentor and good friend.'

'He's going to be alright, Len.'

Lenny wrapped his arms around her weary shoulders.

'Malik's a warrior. I knew he'd be ok.'

He turned and firmly shook the doctor's hand.

'Thank you, doctor.'

'You're welcome sir. I'm just doing my job. He's a lucky young man.'

Jennifer turned to the doctor, worry still firmly in her eyes.

'Can I see him?'

'In a moment, the nurse is just stitching him up. I will call you in shortly.' He disappeared through a set of double doors.

Jennifer folded her arms and turned back to Lenny.

'So what now? This isn't going to stop, is it? I thought Malik had left that life.'

Lenny looked defeated, his mind turning over the event that had just taken place.

'Jennifer, did you see their faces? Height? Anything?' Lenny sounded like an overzealous detective who had just arrived at a crime scene.

'No I didn't see, just heard. But there were at least four of them – oh, and one of them dropped a bandana in the hallway.'

Lenny's eyebrows rose above his glasses. 'Oh? What colour was it?'

Marcia looked to the floor, recalling her memory. 'Green ... bright green.'

The answer pounded Lenny's chest. He couldn't hide the discomfort that had spread across his face. Jennifer had confirmed his worst thoughts.

'D.O.A.,' he muttered under his breath, but loud enough for Jennifer to hear.

'Who is D.O.A. Lenny?'

'A gang from Tottenham sides. It's run by Ninja.'

'Ninja? Who the hell is Ninja?'

'Nathan Lewis-he's the same yout in that mix up with Malik and that Journalist woman. He's in prison now.'

The penny dropped in Jennifer's confused thoughts.

'Oh I see. So what, now he wants to kill my son because he's locked up and Malik's not?'

'Well to be honest, this beef between Malik and Ninja goes way back. It's not really up to me to tell you. So I suggest you speak to your son.'

Jennifer remained silent.

Lenny could feel her affliction, it was written all over her face. She looked troubled and he felt obliged to do something about it.

The doctor reappeared through the swinging

doors with a clipboard. He stopped briefly to tick off some notes and then approached Jennifer.

'Miss Simms, you can come through now.'

Caught in the Cookie Jar

Kia made another futile attempt to squeeze into her slim fit jeans, but her newly formed bump was making it an impossible task. She threw down the jeans and opted for a pair of black leggings and a long chenille jumper, sighing as she admired her beauty in the bathroom mirror.

'Come on girl,' she whispered, giving herself some much needed reassurance. She'd had to develop a courage that was beyond her years. Coming to terms with so much turmoil was testing her resilience beyond its comfortable limits. Her best friend was locked up for smuggling drugs, Malik was stabbed. It came with the territory, but it didn't make it any easier to deal with. She picked up her phone and brought up a picture of herself and Malik on the screen. It was a picture from the school prom. Malik was dressed like a 1930s hoodlum in a dark pinstriped suit, topped with a brimmed hat, finished off with some shiny black and white spats. Kia stood next to him in a sultry blue strapless dress with a

pair of long black velvet gloves and elegant heeled shoes. A tear trickled from the corner of her eyes as she reminisced about the moment she felt like a princess. Malik had told her he would never leave her; he'd looked deep into her eyes like he truly meant it. She wondered whether he was just caught up in all the glamour of the night, or if he felt that way at the time. She slowly massaged her tummy, which began to wrench as more tears began to flow.

'Kia, are you ok in there?' Angela shouted from the passageway. Kia took some slow deep breaths before answering.

'Yeah Mum, I'm ok ... just can't believe I'm having a baby,' she lied.

She walked back to her bedroom, sat down on the bed and squeezed on a pair of Ugg boots. She then opened her handbag and pulled out a brown envelope to check over the visiting order that she'd received from Aisha.

A December chill had brought an overnight sheet of snow that had lightly settled on the balcony outside the window. Kia got up and looked across the estate at the old weathered bricks and rows of blue balconies that were in much need of a lick of paint. Down below two young boys were trying to make snowballs of the little snow available. Kia pictured Malik pushing their child on a swing at the bottom of their own garden, somewhere far from the gloomy scene down below.

That's all I want, she thought before closing the curtains. She put on her quilted jacket and turned up the fur collars to shield her face from the cold. Months earlier she had sold her faithful Vauxhall Corsa to buy a cot, pushchair and some other baby necessities. Malik had failed to come forward with any financial support, choosing to ignore the whole saga like it was a bad dream. He'd even refused to allow her to visit him at the hospital, not wanting her to see him looking vulnerable.

Kia's phone began vibrating on the bedside cabinet. She picked it up and hesitated when she saw 'Unknown' flashing on the screen

'Hello.'

'I told you,' a male voice barked down the line.

'Yuh didn't do duh right thing like I said, did you? Bare trouble now, yuh get me. I told you.'

'Look, get off my phone,' Kia snapped. 'Don't call my phone again you—'

The line went dead. Vexed, Kia picked up her handbag and exited the flat. The threatening phone calls were persistent and she desperately wanted to tell Malik, but his coldness had left her shivering.

A group of lively school children congregated around the bus stop. Some were noisily darting in and out of the corner shop. Jennifer stood observing the young black female who was standing just in front of her. She recognised the petite, shapely figure, even from behind.

'Kia.'

Kia turned around and instantly broke into a wide smile.

'Oh my days! Jennifer.'

Jennifer stepped forward to embrace her, not noticing her protruding stomach.

Kia held Jennifer at a safe distance.

'Careful.'

Jennifer looked down.

'Oh *wow* ... you're pregnant.'

'Yep!'

Jennifer saw the water welling up in Kia's eyes.

'What's the matter? Don't tell me the boy's left you ... who is he?'

Kia was incensed.

'What do you mean? It's Malik's.'

Jennifer's concerns deepened.

'What? How come I didn't know about this? Malik told me that you guys split up because you were not getting on, he said nothing about you being pregnant.'

Jennifer placed her hand on Kia's shoulder.

'Why didn't you call me?'

Kia wiped a tear away with her gloved finger.

'I thought you knew. I was upset because you ain't called me or anything, you've been a better mum to me than my own mother.'

'Oh darling, don't say that.'

'It's true though. You have been.'

'What's your mum saying about this?'

'Well, she's kind of fixing up now, since I told her about Aisha going prison, it's like she saw the light or something.'

Jennifer raised an eyebrow.
'Aisha?'
'Yeah, mixed girl, I brought her round yuh house a couple times.'
'Oh yes, very pretty girl.'
'Yeah, I'm going Holloway now to see her.'
The bus pulled into the bus stop.
Jennifer summoned Kia to get on.
'We'll talk on the bus.'

'Malik, you finished that exhaust yet mate?'
'Nearly boss, I'm just tightening duh back box.'
'Ok mate, when you've finished I wanna word in the office.'
'Damn,' Malik mumbled under his breath, unsure about what was on Tony's mind.
'Ok boss.'
He slowed down the pace on the spanner, drawing out the job while he mulled over recent events. After the last bolt was tightly secured, he strolled over to the sink to wash the thick grease from his hands. Flashes of the attack came flooding in, making him press his lips tightly together in an attempt to suppress the vengeful urges that were occupying his mind.
'Try kill me in my own yard yuh know. I ain't having it.'
The words barely filtered through his gritted

teeth.

After drying his hands, he took a deep breath before heading towards the office. His mobile began vibrating deep inside his overalls which stopped him in his tracks as he animatedly dipped his hand into several pockets until he located it. 'Mum calling' flashed up on the screen.

'Mum, what's up? I'm just about to go into the boss's office.'

'What's up?' Jennifer shouted. 'How the hell you go and get that poor girl pregnant and just leave her to deal with it? I raised you better than that. Why did you not tell me?'

'Ah Mum man! Who told you?'

'Does it matter who told me? I want to know exactly when you were going to tell me that I'm about to be a Grandmother! How could you be so cold? I saw Kia this morning at the bus stop — sold her car and everything to get things for the baby.'

Malik paused, ashamed.

'What?!'

'What, is that all you got to say? Look, now is not the time, but we'll talk about this when you get home.'

'Alright Mum, I hear you.' Malik hung up before Jennifer could say goodbye. He let out a heavy breath, then strolled through the reception area, noticing that Zoe was not present. He knocked the office door.

'Come in mate.'
He cracked open the door and stepped inside.
'Where's Zoe, boss?'
'Oh, I gave her a couple days off to take care of her horses. Her stable girl's done a sickie. Anyway, sit down mate.'

Malik pulled out a wooden chair from under the huge Georgian desk, his eyes scanning the plush office. He zoned in on a large glass display cabinet full of bodybuilding and boxing trophies which fitted a few more pieces to the jigsaw about his boss's past. Tony sank into the thick leather hide of his vintage chair. He swivelled from left to right, studying Malik's face.

'Relax, you look nervous.'
'Nah boss, just wondering what yuh wanna talk to me about.'

Tony locked his hands together and placed them on the desk.

'What happened that night?'
Malik shuffled uncomfortably on the chair.
'I don't really wanna talk about it boss.'

Tony stared directly into Malik's eyes; he could see that the ordeal had shaken him.

'Alright mate, another time ... Lenny told me you gave a lot more than you got though. You're obviously a lot harder than I gave you credit for.'

Malik shrugged.
'Survival, innit!'

'That's it, mate. If you're gonna go out, go out fighting. That's an East End motto mate.'

Tony leaned sideways and removed a square brown paper package from his drawer and placed it on the desk.

'Right, you look like you need some fresh air, so you're gonna do a little errand for me. You see this package; it's worth a lot of money. Now there's a moped at the back of the garage, it belongs to my nephew.'

He reached under the desk and produced a crash helmet.

'Here take this, and here's the address.'

He handed over a piece of crumpled paper.

'It's Zoe's old man's house. Zoe will be there, she's expecting you.'

Malik studied the package and was almost certain of what it contained, but dared not ask. Tony was a very serious man, and Malik was zealous to please him. He looked at the address.

'This sounds far boss.'

'Colchester mate. You need to get out more, explore a bit. There's a big world out there ... being stuck on that bloody estate won't teach you anything.'

'Alright, but how do I get there?'

'Take the sat nav out my motor and stick it in your pocket.'

Malik got up and then reached out to pick up the package. Tony put a huge hand on top of Malik's, pinning it and the package to the surface. He then looked up at Malik.

'Drop this off, no questions. And before you go, if things get on top with this Ninja geezer, you let me know, His old man is a nasty bit of work.

Malik felt slight discomfort, but agreed anyway.

'Ok boss, will do.'

The wet road surface prompted Malik to ease off the throttle as he cornered the winding country lane leading to the village. Up ahead, a red tractor came trundling towards him. Across a field to the right he spotted a large wooden windmill; this was the landmark he'd been looking for. After taking the next right turn, he twisted the throttle back as far as it would allow, letting the 50cc engine screech to its limits. A flock of starlings took flight from a nearby hedge, startled by the noise as Malik raced through the narrow lane towards the cottage behind the windmill. Turning onto the gravel pathway, he coasted past a couple of small barns and then up the driveway of an ample sized thatched roof cottage. Removing the helmet, he admired the surroundings and cut the engine. The cottage door opened and Zoe appeared, dressed in beige jodhpurs and a loose checked shirt. Her blonde hair was tied up in a bun, which made her blue eyes shine out from her lightly tanned skin. She broke into a wide smile.

'Hello, Trouble.'

Malik smiled back.

'Yuh alright, Zo?'

She pushed the door open, then disappeared down the hallway.

'Come in then.'

Malik checked that the package was secure down the front of his jeans; then entered the cottage.

'I'm in here,' Zoe shouted from the kitchen.

Malik walked through the open door into a large kitchen, which had handcrafted oak units and a huge green six-burner cooker. The floor was dressed with large natural stone tiles, which complimented the terracotta wall tiles.

Zoe stood by the sink filling a kettle with water.

'Wanna cuppa?'

'Yeah, that'll be good, my hands are freezing.'

Malik sat down at the dining table and didn't take long to notice Zoe's curvy shape and firm buttocks, accentuated by her tight riding bottoms.

'Right. The kettle's on. You got the package?'

'Yeah, it's here.'

Malik slid it across the table. Zoe examined it; then put it down, looking into Malik's vacant eyes.

'Malik, what's wrong?'

'Nothing Zo, I just got tings on my mind.'

'Got tings on yuh mind,' she mocked.

Malik arched his eyebrows, unimpressed.

'Don't take liberties.'

'I'm not. Take a chill pill.'

She stirred the two cups of tea, added some biscuits on a saucer and placed everything on a tray.

'Come on, follow me.'

Zoe left the kitchen and walked across the hallway into the living room. Malik caught sight of a framed picture on the wall next to the living room door of a dark haired burly man in a green Barbour coat with a cocked shotgun resting over his forearm. On the ground were a couple of dead pheasants and a golden retriever standing loyally at his side.

Malik studied every detail of the print.

'Dis is your dad innit?

Zoe chuckled from the adjoining room.

'Nah, it's Sylvester Stallone. Of course he's my dad.'

Malik kissed his teeth.

'Whatever, man.'

He joined Zoe and sat down on the sofa, making a deliberate effort not to invade her personal space. He looked at the exposed beams and then across at the fireplace which was crackling away, bringing what felt like a different kind of warmth to the room.

'Rah, dis is proper cosy.'

He felt relaxed. In a strange way he felt safe in this environment he knew little about.

Zoe broke the moment's silence.

'What's it like where you live?'

Malik sipped his tea.

'It's grimy.'

'What's grimy? I don't understand.'

Malik snapped his head around.

'You just don't get it ... living large in yuh big houses, bunning money on horses and Range Rovers like it's nuttin. I gotta wake up every day in some damp dingy arse flat and have to be watching my back so I don't get caught slipping. And look what happened ... I get rushed in my own yard ...'

Malik paused and took another swig of tea.

'You wanna know about grimy? Come live where I live.'

Zoe moved up closer and placed her hand on Malik's knee.

'Why are you so angry? I'm sorry ... it's not my fault that I've got this life. I'm 21 and I don't know anything really, my mum and dad kind of sheltered me. They sent me to boarding school and then University. I've only mixed with rich white kids.'

Malik sighed, realising he'd exposed his inner grievances.

'Sorry Zo.'

He looked at her. She looked innocent and quite naive.

'Tings are getting to me; I mean I was lucky they didn't stab me in my chest or suttin. It's not jus dat anyways. My ex-girl is pregnant, now my mum's on my case.'

'Why is your mum on your case?'

'Cos I left her innit. I'm not ready for dat right

now, man'z gotta make peas … Datz money, before yuh ask another stupid question.'

Zoe moved her hand up Malik's knee and gently caressed the top of his thigh.

'Do you love her?'

'Yeah I kinda do, but I got things I need to deal with.'

He ignored Zoe's hand. It was relaxing him and it felt good.

'The closest I've come to a black guy is … well actually, I've never met one. Well not until now anyway. You kind of remind me of that boxer …'

'Well, whoever you're thinking of – he ain't got nuttin on me.'

Zoe playfully nudged him in the side.

'Alright, show-off.'

Malik winced.

'What's wrong?'

'My cut, man'z delicate yuh know.'

'Can I see it?'

Malik thought about her request, he sensed she was getting into him.

'Alright, a quick look yeah. Dis ain't no museum ting.'

He removed his hooded sweater and leaned back on the sofa.

'Look then.'

Zoe gently lifted up his white vest, revealing the inch and a half wound which was now scabbed over.

'When did the stitches come out? It looks really sore.'

'Last week, innit.'

Zoe jumped up.

'Stay there, I'm coming.'

She strolled across the hallway back into the kitchen.

Malik put his feet up and lay back on the sofa. A million thoughts raced through his mind like a herd of gazelles. He let them pass and then blocked them out; he felt like he was in a sanctuary and wanted to stay in it as long as he possibly could. Zoe soon returned with a bowl of ice and knelt down on the floor. She slid Malik's vest up his torso as far as his chest, struggling to contain the sensual feelings as she gently lowered a piece of ice onto the wound.

All Malik's inhibitions about white girls disappeared as she glided the cube across to his navel area. He clenched his left fist as a mixture of coldness and arousal overcame his body. Zoe removed her shirt; then expertly began teasing Malik's lips with the ice.

'Open your mouth,' she whispered.

Malik obliged as she softly kissed him. He closed his eyes, breathing in the fragrance of Chanel.

She got up from the floor and straddled his lower stomach, then eased her hands up under his clothing to his chest, biting her lip as she felt the firmness of his body.

Ronnie steered his black Range Rover onto his driveway, his mobile phone lodged between his shoulder and his face.

'So, did you get the sample?'

'Yeah, I did and the rest of the gear is in transit.'

'Right, that's great. Well I've just got back to my gaff - Left the gym early mate - I was feeling a bit knackered ... just pulling up now. Hold on a minute, what's your Tommy's moped doing on my drive?'

At the other end of the phone line, Tony was puzzled. 'What are you on about?'

'His bike's on my drive mate.'

'Oh shit, Ron, I forgot. I sent Malik round your house with the sample.'

'So what's he still doing here then?'

'How the hell do I know? Maybe he stopped for a piss.

'Tony, I'll call you back.'

Ronnie hung up and got out of the vehicle; the worst case scenario had already entered his head and clouded his thoughts with a red haze that sent him rushing towards the house like a raged bull. Noticing the front door was ajar, he pushed his way in.

'Zoe,' he shouted.

There was no reply, but he could hear sudden movement coming from the living room.

'That little black ...' He didn't finish his sentence,

rushing towards the living room door.

Zoe panicked.

'Hold on dad.'

But all 18 stone of her father came crashing through the door, almost removing it from its hinges.

'What the hell's going on here?'

Zoe frantically tried to cover her nakedness with whatever cushions she could grab. Terror gripped her face as her father bowled towards Malik, who had just managed to pull up his jeans.

'Boss, hold on...!

The words barely left his mouth. Ronnie was on him, pushing him backwards and pinning his neck down into the sofa.

'Dad, don't hurt him ... please,' Zoe screamed into deaf ears.

'Touch my daughter? Are you off your head mate?'

Malik gasped for air, his neck entrapped in a vice-like grip. He could see every particle of Ronnie's hate-filled eyes peering down at him. *I'm dead*, he thought. *It's all over.*

Ronnie squeezed tighter.

'No man touches my daughter, especially not your sort. Do you know who I am? Ronnie bloody Brookes, mate.'

Zoe clambered back into her clothes.

'Dad, stop ... pleeaassse.'

Malik tried in vain to remove Ronnie's hand,

kicking to free himself. His blood vessels burned inside his head, he began to feel faint. Ronnie's phone began ringing on the floor; it had fallen out of his pocket in the struggle. Zoe scrambled for it in desperation, seeing Tony's name flashing up on the screen. He had put two and two together.

Zoe yelled into the receiver,

'Tony, my dad's got Malik!'

'Put the phone on loud speaker.'

Zoe promptly complied and pressed the button.

'Ronnie!! Let him go mate, he's a good kid.'

Malik's eyes began to fade. Zoe was now climbing the walls.

'Tony, he's killing him!'.

'Ronnie let him go ... do you wanna do bird for some kid, you crazy sod?'

Zoe pulled at her dad's collar.

'Think about Mum, Dad.'

Ronnie paused briefly; then begrudgingly released his grip. Malik coughed violently as he rolled off the sofa onto the floor, clutching his throat.

Zoe rushed to comfort him.

'Malik, are you ok?'

He couldn't answer; he struggled to breathe.

Zoe rubbed his back, which seemed to make things worse.

'I'm sorry, it's my fault...' She threw a hateful glare at her father. 'You almost killed him, Dad. Are you crazy or something?'

Ronnie pointed towards the door, completely ignoring her.

'Get your stuff and get out my house before I do something I regret.'

Malik reached for the remainder of his clothes, still gasping for air.

Ronnie picked up his phone, slowly putting it to his ear as he watched Malik falling over himself to vacate the place. Ronnie turned his attention back to his friend, calmly wiping his forehead with the back of his hand.

'Tony, I'll meet you at yours later, we gotta talk some business.

'Alright mate, now calm down, I'll handle dis.'

Warning Signs

Joyous voices harmoniously injected some much needed soul into a hymn that, quite frankly, belonged in St Paul's Cathedral. The cold church hall progressively began to warm up, as the song flowed into glorious heights. A congregation of predominantly West Indian heritage began to sway to the groove of the musicians. This was a new church, modern in every way. The tambourines and wide brimmed church hats had long been replaced by a funky drummer, a keyboardist and a youth who wouldn't look out of place on a tough estate, strumming the bass guitar. At the front, Pastor Denton steadied his laptop on the ornate altar and began searching for his prepared sermon.

In the back row Malik and Tubbs tried to stay inconspicuous. Tubbs had grown up in church. His Nigerian mother would literally drag him along the pavement when he'd refused to go as a youngster and he still had the scarred knees to show for it. Malik nervously fiddled with his BlackBerry. Unlike Tubbs, he hadn't been in a church since the day the vicar had almost drowned him in holy Evian water, when he was just five months old. But things had drastically changed since then. There were a few youths in amongst the adults who looked like him, adorning street swagger in its full glory and looking comfortable doing it. Malik sat observing, this was not the brimstone and fire mayhem he had conjured up about church. Jennifer had coaxed him to come after a lifetime of avoidance, stating it would make her feel a whole lot better after a crazy few weeks.

'I Give Myself Away' faded out into the distance as the pastor took his place. Malik looked on in awe, he wasn't the old school balding Jamaican he expected, but a trendy well-groomed gentlemen in his late 40s, possibly early 50s, who looked like he still had some street credential. Standing 6ft plus, even the people in the back row could see his fresh level one fade. The pastor adjusted his designer glasses.

'Good morning church ... any reggae fans among us?'

Silence descended on the congregation as denial took its place, apart from a few hesitant hands that were barely visible above the many heads.

'Now I know there are more of you than that... come on now, this music is our culture. Some of the most spiritual men in the world were and still are reggae artists. This brings me onto my sermon for today...Signs.'

The congregation looked on, clearly not sure where he was heading.

'Yes, you heard right...I said *Signs*. Like the late great Tenor Saw once sang,

The pastor held the microphone close to his lips

and broke into a song in his usual humorous style:

'Life is one big road, with lots of signs, signs and more signs ... I'm gonna make up my mind to face reality all the time ... yeah.'

Within seconds the congregation was hooked. Malik disengaged from his mobile phone; the pastor had got his attention, although he would probably never admit it to himself, let alone anyone else. He was beginning to warm to the down to earth dude at the altar.

'Signs...are you with me people?'

'Yes, Pastor!'

'When I was a young boy growing up I saw a lot of signs. Like when my mudder told me to tidy my room and she gave me that look...you know the look I'm talking about. And in all mi wisdom, I decided I was not tidying my room until I was ready. You know what happened? Di door fly open and she buss mi backside...'

Belly felt laughter erupted through the congregation. The pastor waited, timing his words to perfection.

'From that day, I knew dat look, was ah *warning sign*.'

A shout of *Amen* came from somewhere deep in the middle section. Jennifer turned around to see if Malik was paying attention. She gave her son a half smile, which he returned. Pastor Denton briefly looked down at the screen.

'Now there are *warning* signs everywhere ... like if you're driving down the road and you see a sign saying 'No Right Turn; it's there for a reason, people. Because if yuh tek dat turn...' He paused. 'You will mash up di car.'

Laughter erupted through the church for a second time, this time deeper than the first. A couple of elders in the front row began fanning themselves as they struggled to contain their delight for the young pastor. The cold chill had now dissipated from the building. Pastor Denton looked around, proudly admiring his mix of people all sitting in anticipation. He lowered the microphone to chest level.

'God is showing us signs every day, not because he wants to be annoying and get us vex. It's because he knows that certain roads will lead us to destruction. Maybe if that burglar did pay attention to the picture of the Pit Bull Terrier in the front window before he decided to bruk in and teef ... he wouldn't have get yam by di darg...' The pastor chuckled, amused by his own humour.

'Some signs are not so obvious, but the word of God will give you the wisdom to recognise the signs that he is showing you. Now let us turn our bibles to Proverbs 20: 21. Read for me please, Sister.'

Pastor Denton motioned to a short greying lady sitting in the front row. She stood up and faced the congregation, clearing her throat before reading:

'An inheritance quickly gained at the beginning, won't be blessed in the end. Don't say, "I will pay back evil." Wait for Yahweh, and he will save you...'

Like a vine, the words wound through the church and wrapped around Malik's chest, awakening his sleeping conscience. Tubbs had dozed off into a light sleep, he had played Xbox and smoked herb until the few birds that frequented the estate began singing outside his window.

Butterflies began dancing around in the pit of Malik's stomach. The next day was a do-or-die day. He had rescheduled the robbery after the last plan was derailed by D.O.A., but this time was desperate after Tony had told him to take time out after the whole saga with Zoe. Ronnie had also called that morning and told Tony if he saw Malik again, he would kill him. Malik didn't need any further prompting and removed his overalls, grabbed the few tools he possessed, and left the garage. Since then, the walls of his small bedroom seemed to be closing in and suffocating his options. With Kia ready to give birth at any moment and the mounting pressure from his mother, the wide road was beginning to look very narrow. Jennifer felt that Kia was a positive influence on Malik, she couldn't understand why he'd let such a kind spirited girl go.

Malik began to second guess himself; he nudged Tubbs who slowly opened his eyes. Malik leaned over and whispered.

'Tubbs, yuh ready to make dis paper?'

'Of course blud. Why? You changing yuh mind?'

Malik briefly looked down towards the front of the church.

'Nah man, it's just suttin the pastor said … don't worry about it, we're rolling same way yeah.'

Tubbs gave Malik a searching look. The two youths then touched fists to seal the agreement.

The silver VW Scirocco seduced every materialistic fibre in Tempo's body. Running his fingers over the glossy spread and across the streamlined bodywork, he imagined himself leaned back behind the steering wheel cruising down Kingsland High Road. An imaginary bass line rumbled in his head as he took a slow pull on his spliff. A large poster of a heavily tattooed basketball player stared down from his grey bedroom wall. On the opposite wall his collection of baseball caps hung unevenly on the crooked nails just above a small chest of drawers. He scanned the room and thought about redecorating and making it a bit plush. Reaching over to the bedside cabinet, he picked up a small framed picture of his late brother and kissed the glass.

'Gonna make dis paper, bruv.'

His younger brother, who was a talented football player, was murdered and he strongly suspected the Milly Boys, although it had never been proven.

Inside, his gut began to twist as the painful memory of his brother dying in his arms played vividly in his head like a silent movie. The movie soon faded into a sea of blood, clouding his inner vision.

'Bastards!!'

He threw the frame onto the bed and then punched the wall. Grabbing his mobile, he stood up and dialled Malik.

'Wha gwaan Tempo, yuh ready for dis?'

'Yeah blud, more than ever. Tings are jus emotional right now, yuh get me?'

'You don't sound right, maybe we should laow dis ting. Every man'z gotta be focused, we can't mess up blud.'

'Nah I'm cool, jus miss Carl. Dem Milly Boys need to get shanked.'

'Tempo, I hear you, but we ave to put dat move on duh back burner.'

'I hear yuh, blud,' Tempo reluctantly agreed.

'Hear what, duh plan stays the same, 9.30... lick duh place, in and out. Split up and back to duh meeting point...no long ting.'

'Yeah, let's do dis, blud ... tired of being broke.'

'Alright, later.'

Malik hung up. He gathered the sledgehammers and balaclavas from under his bed and put them in a rucksack. Out in the corridor the front door opened and closed, signalling Jennifer's exit. Malik picked out a pair of black jogging bottoms and a black hooded sweater from his leaning wardrobe. DMX's *One More Road* boomed out from the speaker, feeding him with adrenaline as he slipped into his clothes. A scheduled alarm played out from his phone, as his 8am checkpoint. He put it on snooze, ready to leave on the next alert. After a final check in the mirror, he slipped on a pair of black leather gloves. The vibration from his phone alerted him to an incoming call. *Kia* flashed up on the screen.

'Nooo!! Not now.'

Hesitancy trembled through his thumb as it hovered over the receive button until he eventually answered.

'Kia, what's up?'

'Malik...'

'Wot, man?'

'I'm having the baby.'

The revelation stopped him in his tracks.

'Wot, now...?' He tried to bring some clarity to his scrambled thoughts.

Kia was breathing erratically.

'Malik, please ... come to the hospital. Malik ... if you love me, you'll come.'

Malik heard a female voice instruct Kia to switch off her phone. The line went silent, leaving him rooted to the spot. An internal battle began to rage; his heart began to defeat his mind, but his mind, focused on instant riches, began to gallantly fight back. Am I dis cold? He walked over to the window and looked outside to remind himself of why he was risking everything. The Pastor's words came to him like a whispering breeze and then disappeared. His alarm began to beep on his phone.

'Whyyyy?' he shouted deep from his stomach.

Silencing the alarm, he dialled Tubbs'. Tubbs answered immediately, he was ready and waiting for the go ahead.

'Tubbs, change of plan.'

Tubbs was startled.

'What yuh mean, change of plan?'

Malik got impatient.

'Just listen ... Kia's having the baby right now. I gotta go down there blud. It's kinda cold if I just leave her by herself man.'

Tubbs paused to think.

'Nah, I hear dat.'

'You man go widout me. Call Stuart and Tempo and tell dem wha gwaan.'

'Alright, cool.'

Tubbs! Good luck man.'

'Laow duh sentimentals man, later.' Tubbs hung up.

M alik sat in the corridor, trying to make sense of his turbulent life. Only the sound of oncoming footsteps brought him back to earth.

'Do you want to come in, sir?'

Malik looked up at the female doctor.

'Nah I'm cool thanks, I'll wait out here.'

'The poor girl's been in labour for several hours now and she's been calling for you the whole time. Ok, her mum's in there now, but I think she really wants you there.'

Malik sighed, chewing on the doctor's words. She reminded him of his science teacher with her long silver hair tied back in a ponytail, exposing her pointed features. She moved her hand down and grasped Malik's wrist.

'Come on young man, you may never experience this again.'

Malik put his stubbornness to rest and lazily followed her into the room. Angela looked up as Malik entered and fired a dagger from her eyes that nearly sent him straight back through the door. One glance at Kia's agony-stricken face was enough for him to stay put. He made his way to the other side of the bed and sat on the plastic chair. He grasped Kia's hand and held it tight. She turned her head towards him and just managed a smile. The smell of bodily fluids mixed with clinical hygiene hovered under Malik's nose, adding to his discomfort.

The midwife stroked Kia's forehead.

'Come on darling ... I want another big push.'

'I can't!' Kia yelled.

'Yes you can, dear. Your young man's here now.'

Angela fired another dagger at Malik, but this one missed. He wasn't paying her any attention.

Kia dug deep into her last reserves of strength and pushed.

'Maliiik!' She screamed out, crushing his hand with agonizing strength. Her lifeless body then sank down into the bed. Malik looked at her; she looked beautiful, even in her distressed state. Silence filled the room until a loud wail pierced the air as the midwife lifted a crying baby out from Kia's lower regions.

'Oh my gosh,' Kia sobbed.

'It's our baby, Malik.'

Angela kissed Kia's cheek, while the midwife cleaned up the new arrival.

'Look at you ... well done.'

Angela revelled in the first glance of her grandchild.

'What is it, Mum?'

'It's a boy, darling.'

Malik got up in a trance-like state and headed towards the door. He turned around briefly to catch a glimpse of the new life that had just entered into his confused world.

He then exited into the corridor, exhaling a sigh of relief as the door swung shut behind him. Digging in his pocket, he found his phone, which was on silent. There were nine missed calls.

A news broadcast caught his attention as it echoed out from a small radio behind the information desk.

'*... The Police have cordoned of Chelsea Bridge Road after an incident, which happened at approximately 9.35am this morning. Also today, the London Mayor will be announcing new initiatives to tackle knife crime in the capital after...*'

Malik's heart began to double beat as the words sank in. He paced down the corridor past the vending machine until a signal appeared on his phone screen. Fumbling through the missed calls it soon became apparent that most were from Tempo. He pressed dial and waited. Tempo answered after two rings.

'Murkz, I bin calling you blud.'

'Kia had duh baby, innit. What happened? I heard suttin on duh radio bout Chelsea Bridge. I thought you man got caught.'

Tempo went silent, his breathing was irregular.

'*Murkz...*' He sounded sombre.

Malik got anxious.

'Wot man?'

'*Tubbs is dead ... He's gone, blud.*'

Mental Warfare

She stood in the doorway, fixated on the empty room. It was still untidy, just the way he left it most days. Now it just seemed all so insignificant. Tubbs was not coming home. A mountain of CDs lay sprawled across the carpet and his battered headphones dangled from his mixing desk, which was still quietly humming. He'd forgotten to switch it off before he left. She'd cursed him every day about the same thing, but now she was left with just a vacant room. It still smelt like an underground dungeon, full of mouldy socks and an overflowing ashtray. She covered her nose, wanting to crack open the window but just couldn't bring herself to step inside and invade his privacy. What privacy? She thought. My boy is not coming back.

Tubbs wanted to be a deejay and had been polishing his mixing skills for a talent competition hosted by a community radio station. A hard slamming on the letter box alerted Christine's attention and reminded her that she needed to get the doorbell fixed. She took one more glance and then shut the door.

'Miss Oleyu, can you open the door please,' a raspy male voice shouted through the letterbox.

She shuffled her plump frame to the door and put a squinted eye to the spy hole. She could just make out two casually dressed white gentlemen peering back at her.

'If you're bailiffs, move away from my door ... I am not paying you anyting.' Her strong Nigerian accent had a tone of non-compliance.

'It's the police.' The taller of the two held up an ID badge. Christine cracked open the door, keeping the security chain in place. A hand reached into the gap, brandishing a prestige looking identification.

'CID, it's about Michael. Can we come in, love?'

'Oh I am sorry ... I thought you were bailiffs.'

Christine unhooked the chain and welcomed the two men in the house.

'Come through to the living room, please.'

She disappeared into a doorway adjacent to the bathroom.

They followed her in, taking mental notes as they strolled through the dimly lit corridor.

The shorter officer with a *Jack-the-Lad* persona spoke first.

'Nice house you got 'ere, luv; a lot nicer than that dump of an estate at the back there.'

Christine half smiled.

'Housing Association. I was lucky to get out from that estate. I lived there for 10 years ... and who are you?'

'Sorry luv, I'm Detective Inspector Thompson

and this is my colleague, DC Matthews.'

'She shook his outstretched hand and then sat down on the armchair, gesturing towards the large leather sofa opposite her.

'Please, sit down.'

Matthews sat down first, his fiery ginger hair and faded freckles somehow made him look younger than he probably was. Thompson joined him and took out a notepad from his inner jacket pocket.

Christine looked longingly into Thompson's piercing green eyes.

'What happened to my son?'

He scribbled a few notes before answering.

'That's why we're here, Madam.'

'Now I know that you've had a couple of constables round when it first happened and I know they were a bit reserved with the information.'

'Yes, they just said that there was an accident and my son crashed his moped. The thing is my son didn't have a moped, this is very confusing.'

Thompson leaned forward on the chair.

'Truth of the matter is your son was involved in a fairly high profile armed robbery...'

Christine pointed to herself, shocked at what she had just heard.

'My son, robbery and guns? You can't be serious.'

Matthews interrupted sharply.

'Well not exactly. Michael had a machete.'

Christine gasped.

'Jeezus.' She began fanning herself with an old magazine that she'd picked up from the side table.

Thompson gave her a moment before continuing.

'Anyway, the jewellers that they robbed alerted the police and we had a response unit over there in minutes. Your son sped off towards Chelsea Bridge, pursued by a squad car. Seems like he panicked and went straight through a red light at a main junction ...'

Thompson paused as every painful word impacted Christine's emotional threshold. She waited for what seemed forever for the words to leave Thompson's lips.

'Sorry Madam, he had no chance. The lorry driver didn't even see him; it happened so quickly.'

Christine put her face into her hands and began to rock back and forth.

'But, but,' she stuttered. 'How did this happen? He couldn't have done this by himself.'

'No, he was accompanied by a Tyrone Odoku. Do you know him?

Christine tossed the name around in her head but came up blank.

'Tyrone? I don't think so.'

Thompson checked his watch, like he had somewhere to go.

Matthews dug into his memory for an alias.

'Your son might have called him Tempo...ring any bells?'

'Oh yes ... he came here a few times; a very angry young man.'

'Well, we got him this morning and charged him with armed robbery and various other things. Still won't bring your son back, but at least it'll give you a bit of closure, knowing what really happened that day.'

Christine began breathing heavily; her heart was burning inside. The news was real; real police officers were sitting in her front room. She now knew the circumstances surrounding her son's death and who was involved. Her spirit had never taken to Tempo, she saw him as a loose wire that could spark at any given moment.

Matthews got up and walked across the room and picked up a school photo of Tubbs off the top of a packed bookshelf. He held it towards Christine.

'Is this Michael?'

'Yes, that was when he was in Year 9 ... such a lovely boy.'

Thompson looked across towards the passage.

'Erm, do you mind if we have a look around his room?'

Christine got up from the armchair, angered by the request.

'How can you ask such question? Do have a warrant?'

'Err, not exactly but —'

She pointed towards the living room window.

'But nothing! Leave my house and leave me to grieve for my son.'

Thompson motioned with his head for Matthews to leave. He stopped briefly, fidgeting inside his jacket pocket. After producing a card, he gently placed it on the coffee table.

'If you need anything give me a call.'

Jennifer knocked on the door for the second time, but more threatening bass came rumbling back as a reply.

'Malik, Lenny's here to see you.'

She knocked again, this time with more venom. The door was wrenched open and a disgruntled Malik stood hunched in the doorway, his face screwed to one side.

'Wot?'

Jennifer sighed, shaking her head.

Lenny stepped out from behind the wall.

'Is that how you talk to yuh mum?'

'Oh, what's going on Lenny? I didn't know you were here.' Embarrassment was written all over his unshaven face as he nervously began twisting a lock of hair at the side of his unkempt head.

Lenny studied him for few seconds.

'What, yuh turning Rasta?'

Malik paused.

'Nah man, just can't explain nuttin right now.'

Jennifer threw Lenny a concerned look which

said a lot of things, things that Lenny was anxious to find out.

'Can I come in?'

Malik shrugged.

'In here's messy, but come in still.'

Jennifer made her way back to the kitchen.

'Are you staying for dinner Len?'

'Yeah, but not too much on the plate.'

Lenny subconsciously massaged his stomach.

'Have to save some space. Don't want Marcia cussing me bout nyamming next woman's food.'

Jennifer laughed.

'Okay, I hear you.'

Lenny followed Malik into the dark room and was immediately overwhelmed by the smell of stale food coming from a pile of half-eaten takeaway containers. The blinds were slightly tilted, allowing the slightest strips of light into the darkness. Lenny opened them fully and shifted a pile of clothes off the small chair to sit down.

'What, yuh hibernating?'

Malik looked up, his eyes half open.

'Nah, I've just locked off for a bit.'

'Your mum's worried about you. Said you ain't come out this room for a week now. I know you Malik ... this ain't you.'

'Yuh don't know me, blud,' Malik snapped. 'Yuh don't know what's going on in man'z head right now, it's a madness! I—I—I feel like I'm going mad.'

'Malik calm down. This is an emotional time right now, I know. But let's get tings into perspective.'

Lenny held out his left hand as a calming gesture. Malik jumped up from the bed; a burning rage flickered in his eyes.

'Don't talk to me bout *perspective.* I jus wanna send Ninja to duh graveyard, blud, and all his little wasteman dem. They wanna war, let dem come innit. Try run me out of my own endz ... Are u mad?'

Malik paced up and down, his arms flailing towards the ceiling.

'Tubbs is dead, they got Tempo. Dat coulda been me. Dem man are family, like brothers, yuh get me. What am I supposed to do now Len? You tell me. I got a baby boy to look after; I ain't got nuttin for him. I can't even face Kia, I bopped out duh hospital and I ain't seen her since. Dis is a madness,' he repeated.

Malik pulled off the hooded top he was wearing.

'It's getting hot in here.'

Lenny wisely waited for the debris to settle from the emotional explosion. He vowed to do all he could to save the angry young man in front of him.

'First things first: you need to jump in the shower and shave that carpet of your face. You look like some big tuff back man.'

Malik half grinned, running his fingers across his face.

'Yeah Len, when we done talk.'

Lenny's face changed, Malik knew he was about

to get serious.

'We need to talk some strategies into this situation. Life is never easy but you have to work with what you got and build on it. Send the negatives back where they came from. You understand me?'

Malik slowly lifted up his head and then put it back down.

'If you keep up this angry man ting, you'll end up killing yourself long before Ninja steps to you. That's real talk. I learnt a lot in them years I spent around Tony.'

Malik's ears pricked up at the sound of Tony's name.

'How you know my man anyway? Yuh never told me he's proper gangster. Man'z frightening, blud.'

Lenny undid his top shirt button.

'Open the window and turn down the music a bit. You need to listen to some culture ... Chronixx, Capleton, Sizzla and dem kinda man ... too much of dat *Kill Nigga* music ain't good for the soul. I'll get a CD out the car and give it to you before I leave.'

'Alright cool, but let me hear bout Tony.' Lenny hesitated.

'Basically, when I was about your age I used to drum a few houses. You know that type of thing ...'

He took a long breath and continued.

'Look, the truth is I was hooked on crack ... and one day I decided to travel out the area and I reached clean over Dagenham sides. So I'm burgling this house on one cul de sac ... I was desperate, just needed to get my drugs. So I'm in the bedroom looking for the jewellery and next thing this big guy comes from nowhere. I was cornered and that was it. The man done me, I mean a proper beating. I was in intensive care for weeks. Next thing I know, when I finally got out of there the same man came and offered me a job as a drug runner. Helped me get off the crack and make money from the pure stuff instead. Said he liked a kid who wasn't afraid to take chances. That's how I met Tony. We've been tight ever since. We got some weird mutual respect. But don't get it twisted. He is one dark guy. I have seen things that still haunt me to this day'

Malik focused on Lenny; he could see that the story had brought back some unfavourable memories. He had never heard him struggle to talk. He felt an even deeper respect for the man who had given up his time for him.

'I have seen it and lived it, that's why I am doing what I'm doing. Helping you young men is the cross I have to carry for my sins. I owe it, because frankly, I should be dead.'

Malik extended his fist to meet Lenny's. 'I hear you Len, respect for that man.'

Lenny cracked a smile. 'Bwoy, smell like your mum's food ready. Go hold that shower, so we can eat.'

The two men got up to leave the room, without

discussing Kia, Ninja and all the other issues that had put Malik in a desolate place, where suicidal thoughts were buzzing around his head like a swarm of angry bees.

Ninja in the Dark

The moonlight shone into the darkness of the BMW, deliberately parked under a broken streetlight. A young rat scurried out from a derelict warehouse, then disappeared into dense bushes behind a broken fence. It was quiet for a Friday night; the obscure side street was even quieter. Raymond lit another cigarette and took a hard pull, before blowing out rings of smoke. He checked the time on the dashboard: 10.55pm. A soulful house tune softly caressed the large shelf speakers and he slowly rocked his head to the rhythm. Keeping his eyes focused on his rear-view mirror, he cautiously watched for any sudden movement.

It wasn't long before a pair of car lights beamed around the corner from behind, then dimmed as the car came to a standstill ten yards back. Raymond checked his left wing mirror for a better angle, straining his eyes to identify a dark coloured Ford Focus. A tall hooded figure stepped out from the passenger side and began a lingering walk towards the vehicle. Raymond lowered his baseball cap over his eyes shuffling tentatively in the seat. The

stranger was soon at the window, peering into the darkness of the tints.

Raymond lowered the glass.

'Password mate.'

The dark-skinned youth stared Raymond down for a few seconds.

'*Bethnal*, innit.'

Raymond released the central locking.

'Alright, get in.'

The youth gave another defiant stare before walking around the large saloon and slipping in the passenger seat.

Raymond reached beneath his seat and produced a white cloth wrap.

'Right, let's do some business.'

The youth glanced down, his dark skin and intense eyes lit up as Raymond slipped on a pair of black leather gloves. Very slowly he unravelled the cloth and carefully parted the folds of the fabric corner by corner, revealing a matt black pistol. The youth watched intently, transfixed on the cold steel as Raymond removed its magazine and expertly rolled a handful of bullets through his fingers and pressed them into place. He then nudged the loaded magazine back into position with the palm of his hand and began swivelling the gun from left to right.

'Right, let me give you a quick instructional tour.' He sucked down another lung full of nicotine and then stubbed out his cigarette in the ashtray.

'Beretta 9mm semi-automatic, loaded with six rounds. Now you cock that back here and push it back in like that, that's loaded. Safety off, safety on. Release the magazine. Load it up; push duh magazine back in like dat ... cock it and you're ready to go.'

The youth watched closely as Raymond handled the weapon with raw precision. He wondered how many guns this stony white guy had sold. But thoughts of his intended victim re-entered his mind and his face twisted and reverted back to a sculptured coldness.

Raymond wrapped the weapon back into its cloth.

'Right 300 quid, as agreed.'

The youth's hand disappeared into his front pocket and emerged with several crumpled twenty pound notes. After checking the amount, he handed the cash to Raymond, who in turn handed over the gun.

Raymond adjusted his cap.

'Right, you don't know me and you never seen me before.'

The youth slowly removed his hood to fully reveal his concealed identity.

'Yuh sure I don't know you?'

His eyes were vacant, emotionless as they focused into Raymond's.

Alarm bells of recognition began to ring inside Raymond's head as memories of a young lad riding a BMX outside Baron's house played out in slow motion. He remembered buying him an ice cream on a hot summer day when he had passed by to do some business. Talk about irony, he thought as he observed the youth properly for the first time.

'I thought there was something about you, but I couldn't quite put my finger on it. You're Nathan, right?'

The youth half grinned.

'Yeah that's right, but on road they call me Ninja.'

Raymond watched him in disbelief.

'Blimey, you've got your dad's eyes, cold as ever.' He paused.

'Look, if you don't want your old man knowing about this, that's alright. Just keep my name out of it.'

Ninja dodged Raymond's words and opened the car door, stepping out into a crisp night.

'I ain't no snitch, blud.'

He bent his head sideways and then dissolved into the dark street.

Malik sat on the stairwell waiting for Roman; he'd agreed to meet him, even though they had no allegiance. Roman was a deep rooted member of The Milly Boys, who were almost certainly responsible for at least two recent murders in the area. Everyone knew, but their lips were frozen with fear. Not even the constant heat from the police could melt the icicles that had formed around people's lips. The murders, along with several others, sat gathering dust in the 'Unsolved' file deep in the archives of Scotland Yard.

Malik acknowledged the sound of approaching

footsteps and peered down from the top of the stairs.

'Yes fam.'

Roman threw Malik a defensive stare but soon relaxed. He respected the lone soldier and the way he'd refused to join the gang. After walking up the steps, he touched knuckles with Malik.

'Wha gwaan Murkz?'

As Roman sat down a couple of stairs below him, Malik noticed the deep scar on the left side of his neck.

'Who chop yuh neck, blud?'

Roman shook his head.

'One a dem D.O.A. man dem – a tall yout called Ghost — he tried to stab me in my face, innit. But I dodged duh blade and got chop in my neck. Was lucky doh, coz he coulda cut my throat, yuh get me.'

Malik nodded.

'Yeah, standard.'

Roman paused for thought.

'So Murkz, yuh still don't wanna join us then, we could do wid a man like you. Yuh coming like some *Terminator,* blud ... you one bang up everyting.'

Malik felt uneasiness in his stomach.

'Nah man, you know I don't roll wid no gang, but I might need yuh help.'

Roman tensed with anticipation. Veins began to appear all over his tattooed forearm. Gang life was all he knew. Like Malik, he'd never met his dad and his mother's mental illness made it impossible for her to raise him. He'd been in a care home from the age of 12 and was thrown out of school at 14. Milly Boys were like his extended family.

He swivelled around to face Malik.

'Wot yuh saying, Murkz?'

Malik waited as an elderly lady entered the stairwell. She glanced up, her face twisted with disgust. Malik gave her a knowing grin. She had got him in trouble with the police many times by getting too liberal with his business. After she disappeared along the landing, he turned his attention back to Roman.

'Ninja's on me. I know he dun send his man dem round my yard ... but I know him, he's persistent. He ain't gonna stop until I'm in duh grave blud. I just wanna know if you man will back me if tings get heavy. I ain't looking to dead right now. Got my little boy, yuh understand me?'

Roman stayed silent, contemplating. His shaven head and tattooed neck made him look much older than his 17 years.

'Murkz, yuh dun know already. Milly Boys and D.O.A. are like Israel and Palestine. It's only a matter of time before we have an all-out war.'

It was what Malik wanted to hear.

'So you got my back?'

Roman pressed his fist against Malik's.

'Of course, blud. When you're in a war, sometimes you have to call on allies, innit.'

Malik nodded, pleased but slightly haunted. Roman got up and headed towards the heavy steel door to the block. He pressed the electronic exit button.

'Bell me, yeah.'

'Roman,' Malik called out.

Roman turned and looked back at Malik through glazed eyes.

'Did you lot kill Tempo's little brother?'

Roman's eyes widened; then shrank. He left the block.

Malik got up, now knowing the truth; he began to climb the stairs to his flat. His mind carried him back to a playground fight with Ninja when they were just 13 years old. He had begun seeing Kia and Ninja went berserk, claiming Kia was his girl. Malik had rendered him unconscious with a flurry of punches. Later that day Ninja approached Malik and whispered in his ear, 'I can't beat you now, but one day I will kill you.'

He had said it in such a chilling way that the words had stuck in Malik's head ever since. Those same words were now tormenting him as he tried to steady his shaking hand to put the key in the door. His phone began vibrating in his pocket. By the time he located it, it had diverted to voicemail. Once inside the flat, he went into his room and slipped a Mayfair Light from the box. After lighting the cigarette he sat down, his gut churned with anxiety.

'One robbery and I'm out of here,' he mumbled under his breath.

Ninja's sadistic voice continued to play like a hated song, that wouldn't go away: 'I can't beat you now but one day I'll kill you.' He sucked hard on the cigarette, looking around his bedroom as if his enemies were about to emerge from the walls. He saw the faces of all the people he had robbed, beaten and left for dead, including the Journalist who had bravely fought back after he'd got her handbag but she had clung to her laptop as if her life depended on it.

Why did Ninja go to prison for it? It doesn't make sense, he thought. As he looked around the room his eyes caught sight of the book that Lenny had sent him when he was in prison. It was still sitting on his bedside cabinet, untouched and unread. Putting out the cigarette he sat back down on the worn carpet and slid the book down from his its resting place.

Opening the front cover, he found a message from Lenny:

To Malik (the better of two halves),
Get to know who you are and where you are from. Only then you will be able to break free from this entrapment.

Bless
Lenny.

Skipping the introduction, he anxiously turned to the first chapter. Feeling deeply ashamed that he hadn't treasured his mentor's gift, he began to read.

Chapter 1

The Boy in the Mirror

I walk across this dreary room and stop in front of the long mirror. Before I look into the smeared glass, I ask myself, 'Why am I here?' Outside my window is a cold and violent world that doesn't seem to extend much further than my post code. But this is all I have ever known. This has been my only existence since my father left me and my mother in this decaying concrete prison.

Slowly I peer into the mirror and I am confronted by a scared young man. I look into his sunken eyes and I see a beaten slave, weak and submissive. He seems so insignificant; just an uneducated soul, still dancing and playing the fool for the slave master. His self esteem has been whipped out of existence, never to return.

Hate begins to fill me and the boy in the mirror looks back at me with the same hateful venom. How can I ever respect him, when history told me that he was just a slave and nothing but a slave?

I reject the darkness of his skin like an

unwanted disease, to the point that I could easily murder that boy in the mirror. I feel no love, nor compassion for him. Who is he anyway? I ask myself.

They told me that he was only a low life, street robbing, baby making criminal who was destined for prison or premature death. He's nothing to me, he don't look like the people I see in government, in the courthouse, running big businesses.

Briefly I stop to question my irrational thinking. 'Was he just here for a while, only to die like a dog on the street or to be locked into captivity?' Is he a product of a legacy that has transcended down from our ancestors and now perpetrated by the modern rulers of this world. I leave the mirror and run to the library, there must be something missing. This can't be his destiny, to simply self-destruct and vanish from this planet. All around me, I see young men who look just like him, dying at the hands of other young men; who look just like me.

Do they ask themselves the same questions that I now find myself asking?

Do they too, hate the boy in the mirror?

Malik looked up, slowly shaking his head as the words leaked into his conscience. He closed the book almost in a trance. Grabbing his phone, he checked the time. It was almost 11pm. Over an hour had already passed since the meeting with Roman. It was then that he remembered the missed call.

He checked his voicemail.

'Yo Murkz, it's Sticky-trying to call yuh blood. Listen, I done a ting wid one girl from Tottenham sides. Bucked her at one party, innit. Anyway, she told me dat Ninja's got a Strap and how he's gassing about popping a bullet in yuh head. Real talk ... Bell me as soon as, blud.' The line went dead.

A Bundle of Hope

Kia glanced down at her phone, beckoning Malik to call.

Angela watched from the kitchen doorway, not amused. After finishing her herbal tea she joined her daughter on the sofa.

'He's not going to call. Forget about him.'

Kia exhaled, looking down into the blanket wrap.

'Look at you, pretty boy. Daddy doesn't know what he's missing.'

His eyes were dark like onyx, shone with excitement as the bottle teat teased his lips.

Angela looked on, proudly admiring her grandson.

'Have you got a name for him yet, honey?'

'Daniel, Mum. I'm gonna call him Daniel. It's a bible name, innit.'

Angela nodded her approval.

'Took your time about it though, he's two months old now.'

'Yeah I know, but I wanted Malik to name him.'

Angela placed her arm around Kia's shoulder.

'Look it's his loss. Look at this beautiful little boy.'

'I don't get it though Mum. Malik never met his dad. You'd think he'd wanna do things different.'

Angela reached out.

'Here, let me feed him.'

She took the bottle and gently lifted her grandson out of the basket.

'Go and get some rest, I heard this little one keeping you up all night.

'Yeah, he was waking up every hour. Are you sure Mum?'

'Go on, I've got this.'

Kia was wary of her mother's sudden change after watching her in squalor for years. She'd cut down on the smoking and was making a valid effort at being a supportive mother, but there were still one or two unsavoury characters in her mother's life that kept her on her guard. The baby's arrival had reignited Angela's maternal extinct in a way that Kia had never seen while she was growing up. Kia got up and wrapped her dressing gown round her slender figure.

'I'm gonna lay down.'

Her phone rang, stopping her in her tracks. She answered without looking at the screen.

'Hello.'

Quiet breathing filtered through the receiver; in the background she could hear a dog's muffled barking.

'Hello, who is dis?'

'Are you taking the mick?' A male voice barked down the line. 'Watch what's gonna happen, I told you what you shoulda done.'

Kia slammed her free hand down on the dining table.

'Get off my phone and leave me alone yeah. Yuh keep making threats. Do something, you *wasteman*.' She threw her phone across the room, startling Daniel who began to cry.

Angela resettled him onto the bottle.

'Kia, what's going on? You've been getting those calls for some time. Don't think I haven't noticed.'

'It's nothing, just some stupid boy.'

Angela lowered her eyebrows, not convinced.

'Thanks, Boss.'

Malik finished his phone call, raising his fist in celebration.

'Yes!'

Jennifer looked up from her book, observing her son's jubilance.

'What's that son?'

'Tony just gave me back my job.'

Jennifer broke into a smile.

'Brilliant, I was getting worried. You haven't been outside for weeks.'

'I know Mum, I couldn't face nuthin. You don't understand how it is on road.'

'Try me; you think I don't know about this D. O. — whatever you call them.'

Malik's eyebrows rose sharply.

'Mum, how yuh know about D.O.A?'

'I know it was them who came up into this house and nearly killed you, I know that much.'

'You've been talking to Lenny innit?'

'Well yeah. He said that I should talk to you, give him his dues. He respected your privacy, but at the same time I'm your mother. You can't expect him not to tell me anything.'

Malik nodded.

'Yeah, true. How's the studying going mum?'

'Nice try, Malik. I wanna know what is going on with you. Who's Ninja?'

Malik rubbed his head, his demeanour shifted from jubilant to nervousness.

Jennifer put her book down on the side of the sofa.

'What's wrong son?'

'Mum, I didn't really wanna tell you dis ... but my man's got a strap. Man wants to kill me.'

'Strap ... what are you talking about?'

'A gun mum ... yuh understand me?'

'What ... what have you got into?'

Angered, Malik got up from the sofa and strutted over to the window.

'I ain't got inna nuthin, he's a mad yout. Dis ting has been going on since school days. Most of dem road man can't touch me, but dis yout is straight evil. I'm in a situation now where I might have to—'

Jennifer cut in,

'You might have to what?'

'Look I don't know, I just need to concentrate on something else. If we clash, then it's me or him.'

Jennifer got up to embrace her son, but Malik avoided her outstretched arms.

'I ain't a little boy now Mum, I'm a man. I can handle dis.'

She frowned, lowering her hands to her hips, surprised at his outburst.

'Does Lenny know about this?'

'Lenny don't know bout duh gun ting, but I don't really wanna get him involved.'

'Well I'm going to talk to him. See if he can talk to this Nathan boy.

'Nah Mum, trust me ... he ain't gonna listen to Lenny. He don't respect nuthin or no one.'

Jennifer leaned over and picked up her handbag. She rummaged inside and produced a small brown Bible, intent on throwing everything at the situation.

Flicking through the pages, she settled on *Psalm 31:13*. 'Son, you've got nothing else to lose.' Pointing to the verse, she passed the book to Malik, who sighed with contempt.

He began to read, low and under his breath:

13. For I heard the slander of many, terror of every side,
While they conspire together against me, they plot to take my life.

14. But I trust in you Yahweh. I said. 'You are my God'
15. My times are in your hand.
Deliver me from the hand of my enemies and those who persecute me.
16. Make your face to shine on your servant.
Save me in your loving kindness.
17. Let me not be disappointed, Yahweh, for I have called on you.
Let the wicked be disappointed
Let them be silent in Sheol.

Malik closed the Bible, an eerie silence descended into the room; calm that he couldn't explain. It was different from the rare moments of peace he'd experienced before. The intercom began to bleep, breaking the atmosphere. Malik jumped from his almost trance-like state and went to answer it.

'Hello, who dis?'

'Murkz, it's me, Stuart.'

'Rah. Come up man.'

Malik hadn't seen Stuart since Tubbs' funeral; Stuart had gone back to Northern Ireland to clear his head.

Malik let him in and praised him for his excellent timing.

Seizing the opportunity, Jennifer slipped into the kitchen and shut the door. She picked up her mobile from the breakfast table and called Lenny.

'What's up Jen?'

'I can't talk right now; meet me in the café on Hackney Road.'

'Alright, I'll leave now; I'll see you in about 15 minutes.'

'Thanks Len, I appreciate it.'

Kia gave the swing another push, sending Daniel into a fit of giggles. She glanced over at Malik, who was sprawled out on the park bench lazily dragging on a cigarette. For a second she thought she saw someone move behind a tree a few yards back. On second glance, she saw nothing other than a black bin liner that had got caught on the railings and was blowing in the wind. Turning her attention back to Daniel, she gave him one more big push and smiles as he kicked his feet and giggled through his gapped teeth.

A tan coloured bull terrier came bounding into the children's play area and began darting in and out of the fixtures. Kia instinctively removed Daniel from the swing and encircled him in her arms. As she turned to head towards Malik, she caught sight of a hooded youth in black, approaching from the trees. Words appeared in her mind, but she couldn't speak. The youth was now two yards behind Malik, his arm raised. She put her hand to her mouth and closed her eyes; shock had already rooted her to the spot.

A gunshot rang out and echoed through the park.

'Mallliiikkkk!' she screamed as it was her last breath. She felt someone pulling her away from the confusion.

'Kia! Kia!'

Shaking, she opened her eyes; her mind immediately ran on Daniel. As she focused her vision, she could see Malik peering down into her face.

'Babe, wake up. Yuh dreaming man.'

'What? Malik! Oh my days, I thought you were *dead*.'

'What yuh talking about? I'm here man.'

Kia put her arms around his neck, still not fully awake.

'How did you get in my room?'

'Yuh mum let me in, innit. You've been sleeping for a while still.'

'Where's Daniel?'

'Malik smiled. 'I got little man here.'

He motioned his head towards the side of the bed, where Daniel lay asleep in his Moses basket.

Tears began to well in her eyes as every possible emotion came to her.

'I had a horrible a dream. It felt so real.'

Malik put his arms round Kia's waist and held her tightly. Guilt played on his mind.

'I'm here now babe.'

'Yeah, but are we back together?'

The tears began to stream down her face.

Malik kissed her softly, then laid her back down

on the bed. After removing his t-shirt, he slipped
underneath the covers.

Baron Wasteland

DCS Rogers glared down from his 2nd floor office window, watching streams of 9-to-5 workers mechanically toiling through the city haze. Across the busy street a dispute between the driver of a scaffolding truck and a traffic warden drew his attention as the vexed driver slammed a length of steel piping onto the pavement in protest. Rogers chuckled, amused by the scene, but not so amused with the monotonous picture.

'Bloody rat race.'

He sighed before turning back to his desk, glancing at a portrait of his wife and three children, reminding him why he came to work every morning. But the routine was mundane and job satisfaction had now developed a new meaning. With the government continuing to suffocate the establishment with red tape and bureaucracy, criminals were literally getting away with murder. Months earlier Rogers had decided he wanted a piece of the criminal pie. It looked and tasted much better than the 9-to-5 one with the dodgy pension for dessert. Barrington Lewis was the ideal candidate; he hadn't managed to bring down

Tottenham's most notorious gangster due to the incompetence of the justice system. The thought of a black man barely in his forties with so much money was beginning to disrupt his sleep. He deeply resented the cocky Jamaican to the point that bringing him down wouldn't be enough. Using him as a cash cow suddenly felt like a more satisfying option. His wife Cheryl had warned him to separate work from home life, but his bitterness towards the government and the criminal underworld had already begun to corrupt his once flawless career. Picking up his mobile phone, he scrolled through his call list before dialling.

'Mr Lewis, I think we need to have a little chat.'

'Talk bout wha?'

Baron spat down the other end of the phone line.

'Roger's yuh nah get no more percentage. Mi know it's dat why yuh a call mi … yuh ah try box food out ah mi mout.'

Rogers waited for Baron to finish his rant.

'Box what?'

Baron kissed his teeth. 'Mi … nah … gi … yuh … no … more … money.'

'No more money Lewis? You can't operate your business without me, or have you forgotten?'

'Rogers, come like yuh wan run mi outta business. One minute yuh ah try send mi ah jail and now yuh ah extart mi.'

'Extort you?' Rogers laughed. 'You got a bloody cheek talking about extortion. You've extorted more people than the HM Revenue,'

Baron kissed his teeth for the second time.

Roger's sat down at his desk.

'Anyway, that's not what I called for. Thirty percent is alright for now. I called about your son, Nathan.'

'Wha bout him?'

'You need to keep him on a tight leash. I can't have him going after that Malik fella. Last thing I need right now is another murder. What with the riots, Tottenham is like a beacon at the moment. The media will be on it like flies to—' he broke off. 'You know what I'm trying to say.'

Baron coughed, then cleared his throat.

'Ok ... Mi talk to him.'

'Good lad. Right, now we've got that out of the way you can meet Thompson and Matthews down by the River Lea ... 8pm. They'll give you back your little shipment.'

'Lickle shipment? Yuh ah gwaan wicked. Mi soon—' He hesitated.

'You soon what, Lewis? Remember, who's running the show, unless you wanna end up on a murder charge. After all, we all wanna make money ... don't we?'

'Yeah, yeah ... mi hear yuh. '

Baron cut the call.

Baron strolled into Belmont Travel and took a seat at the first available desk. He lounged in the chair, admiring the coffee-toned agent.

'Can I help you?'

Baron grinned, his mind already drifting away from his travel plans.

'What ah way yuh pretty.'

She half-smiled, unimpressed.

'Thank you, now how can I help?'

'Yes darling, yuh ave any flight available fi go ah Jamaica fi August?'

He scrutinized her fingers as she worked her designer nail tips over the keyboard.

'Name please, Sir?'

'Barrington Lewis ... Dem call mi Baron pon road.'

Thinking his near celebrity status would make an impact, he waited for her reaction. Instead she remained straight-laced and professional.

'Address please?'

Baron paused.

'12 Meadows Crescent. Tottenham, N15.'

'How long are you going for?'

'Me nuh come back fi now. Just keep di ticket open please.'

The agent typed in Baron's details, avoiding his discomforting stare.

'Mi going to build ah big house back ah yard. Yuh would look nice pon di veranda in a nice bikini, sipping champagne, fi real.'

He clocked her name tag for the first time.

'Dionne, wha yuh ah say?'

Rolling her eyes, she hit the enter key on the keyboard.

'I'm married, that's what I say.'

She held out her platinum banded finger.

Baron smirked.

'Dat's alright, yuh can bring yuh husband too, him can wash mi car and run sum errands fe mi.'

She broke into a chuckle, amused by his audacious humour.

'Bwoy, mi did tink say yuh never had no smile,' he teased, chuffed with his icebreaker.

'I'm jus playing wid yuh ... how much fi di ticket?'

She smothered her relief, looking back at the computer screen.

'£649.00, including taxes.'

'Ok, book dat fi mi, mi ah pay cash one time.'

After counting out some used fifty pound notes, he got up and flashed a devious smile, attempting to showcase his diamond tooth. Unimpressed, Dionne handed him a preliminary printout of his booking with a look of distaste.

Baron slipped it into his back pocket and dragged his bruised ego towards the door. Once outside, he scanned up and down the busy High Road trying to recollect where he'd parked his new Lexus. Thoughts of driving it through the bustling streets of Kingston, Jamaica were already seducing his mind. He mentally calculated the value of his consignment of cocaine. It had been a setback, but nothing too detrimental. Business was good. Dodging an oncoming bus he crossed the road, remembering he'd parked on a dead-end side street behind the Iceland. Turning into the narrow side street he walked past several tightly parked cars, checking the time on his Rolex. It was 5.30pm; the sun had vanished behind a mist of grey clouds, making it appear later than it was.

As Baron got closer to his vehicle, he noticed a light blue transit van blocking his car.

He drew car keys out from his jeans pocket.

'Ah wuh do dis eediat.'

Diesel fumes were chugging out from the van. Baron picked up pace, intent on confronting the driver. As he drew near to the side of the vehicle, the side door suddenly burst open, startlingly him. A large framed figure rolled out from the vehicle, causing him to step backwards. Before he could decipher the sudden movement, a hard object pressed into his right cheekbone.

'Don't bloody move.'

Baron froze, as the smell of cold steel tainted his airways. Slowly he raised his eyes above the gun barrel to see a hugely built white man with piercing blue eyes behind a ski mask. Baron's bladder burst, leaving him defenceless.

'Wha ... yuh want ... Bredrin?'

'Shut your mouth and do as you're told.'

Baron heard the driver's door open. He remained still. He could feel someone approaching from the side but kept his eyes glued on the gunman. He felt a large hand squeeze into his left shoulder blade, and then everything went black, as a cloth was put over his head.

'Get in the van.'

A gravelly voice commanded from behind.

Baron tried to control his breathing. He searched his mind for answers. Rogers? It can't be. He thought hard, searching for a motive, but there wasn't one. They had settled things earlier in the day. Baron felt a hard shove in his back which sent him stumbling into the edge of the van; he fell forward onto the cold flooring. Pain ripped through his right thigh as he struggled to get up.

'Grab his legs,' the gunman instructed his accomplice.

Baron felt his lower body being lifted and instinctively cooperated, not wanting to provoke any erratic behaviour. Seconds later the side door slammed shut and echoed through the hollowness of the empty van. Baron could feel the barrel of a shotgun sadistically teasing the side of his face as he sat up against the metal panelling.

'Wha yuh want from mi? Yuh want money? Mi have money.'

His voice was faint beneath the cloth hood.

The gunman prodded the barrel into Baron's

forehead to up the level of fear.

'You'll find out soon enough ... now shut up. I don't wanna hear you.

A list of past enemies began to stack up in Baron's thoughts. But there were too many enemies and just as many victims. The van began to manoeuvre backwards, then slowly forwards. Baron put his head down and wondered whether karma had come to pay him a visit.

She finished reading the letter and lay down on her bunk. A lone tear trickled down her nose, dripping onto the pillow. Unable to contain the whirlwind in her stomach, Aisha began to sob as she recalled the words that her best friend had written. She'd promised Kia that she would be there for her when the baby came, but her love for designer labels had tainted her morality. The smell of money had drawn her into a world that she had no business being in. Kia had often warned her that Ninja was using her, but Aisha was naive and submissive. She loved Ninja's reputation more than she loved herself. It gave her a sense of security, a security that her father had never given her. He'd gone back to Jamaica when she was just 10 years old. She often wondered whether his brief relationship with her mother was just a novelty. He was hardly there.

After taking another admiring look at a picture of Kia's baby, she put it back in the envelope. It would be at least two years before she would get to hold him. Her mind flashed back to the small kitchen in Miami, where a seemingly pleasant woman had coached her to swallow the drugs. What the hell, she thought as she relived the ordeal. It hadn't even occurred to her that she could have died if a single bag had burst. She remembered the immigration officer telling her off as if she was her own daughter. Looking up at a picture of her mother on the wall, Aisha blew a kiss.

'I'm sorry,' she whispered.

The sound of heels clicked past her cell door and she knew what was coming next. She read Kia's name and address on the envelope before lights went out. Her head began to fill with visions of Ninja and Baron laughing, enjoying life on the outside. She could see them sitting smugly in prestige cars, smoking weed and partying without as much as a thought for her, languishing in prison. Snitching would surely bring death to her door, and she knew it.

The thin rope cut into his wrists as he squirmed around on the wooden chair. An unwelcomed smell of horse manure and damp hay lingered in the cold air. The pungent scent slowly teased its way into the darkness of the cloth hood that was still loosely covering his head. He heaved with distaste as the realisation that was far from his concrete metropolis. Nearby he could hear a muffled conversation taking place and then faint footsteps became louder. Gripping his fists tightly, Baron tensed, his mind assaulted by vivid images of a painful death like a slideshow. He began to recognise people he had terrorised, stabbed and shot along the way to becoming the most feared man in North London. He shook his head, trying to shake the images from the picture frame that were tormenting him.

'Right, what we got here Ron?'

The cockney voice didn't sound familiar, adding to the confusion. Baron felt the hood being yanked from his head. He looked up, adjusting his eyes to the dimly lit space. Gazing down on him were two huge middle aged white men dressed in blue boiler suits.

The shorter of the two leaned forward.

'Big, bad Baron...'

Baron looked up at him.

'Who's you?'

'Me? You should know who I am-I'm Tony Chaucer.'

Baron's eyes widened as the realisation of who he was dealing with pressed into his chest.

'Tony? Bomba ... Tony Chaucer. Mi hear bout yuh.' Baron put his head down, wishing the earth would swallow him whole and spit him back out on Tottenham High Road. Tony was a man to be feared, no matter who you were. His name carried more weight than a freight train.

Tony looked at his accomplice and then back at

Baron.

'You wanna introduce yourself, Ron?'

His accomplice stepped forward, producing a heavy steel hammer from behind his back.

Fearing the worst, Baron tried to break free.

'Look, no need fi no violence ... come, we talk bredrin. Mi—'

Before Baron could finish his sentence Ronnie raised the hammer and brought it down.

'Aaaaaargh! Bomba!' Baron's scream echoed off the corrugated roof as the hammer smashed into his knee cap. His head fell forward. He made an involuntary move to tend to his leg, but his hands remained bound behind his back.

Ronnie calmly placed the tool on the bonnet of an unfinished vintage car. He smirked coldly, unmoved by Baron's groaning.

'Right, that's my introduction out the way.'

Baron looked up at Tony, trying desperately to put mind over matter.

'Tony, ah who dis madman?'

'You've just met the Devil's bodyguard ... Ronnie Brookes.' Tony grinned menacingly.

Baron surveyed what looked like a derelict barn that had been converted into a workshop.

'Wha yuh want from mi?'

Tony picked up an old barstool from under a work bench and sat down facing Baron.

'Now a little while back. There was a robbery in

Dagenham … and I was supposed to receive 30 kilos of the good stuff. But it never got to me, because a bunch of Muppets took it upon themselves to shoot my driver, pistol whip my cousin and nick my drugs.'

Baron shuffled around on the chair, trying to limit his discomfort.

'Suh why yuh ah tell mi bout it?'

'I thought you might know something about it. You wouldn't wanna lie to me now, would you?'

Tony glared at Baron.

Baron felt naked, but his pride was battling with his predicament.

Tony prodded a strong finger into Baron's chest.

'Well, what have you gotta say mate?'

'Tony, mi don't know nuttin bout no drugs, suh just let mi go bout mi business,'

Ronnie had other ideas and gave Tony a knowing look.

'I think it's time for a barbecue. What do you think?'

Tony nodded his approval. Ronnie grinned and began rolling up his sleeves. He walked behind a dilapidated car and soon returned pulling a large gas cylinder on a two wheeled barrow. Attached to the cylinder was long orange rubber tubing. Baron watched the big man as he emerged. He could just make out the blow torch attached to the end of the tubing. Fear returned to him, filling his chest cavity. He began to struggle violently to free himself.

'Bredrin, wha yuh ah gwaan wid? Mi name Baron, don't bomba play wid me.'

Ronnie laughed.

'You listening to this? He's found his balls'

Tony shrugged his shoulders.

'I think you need to remind him where he is, mate.'

Ronnie pulled the equipment up close and personal. With a quick flick of his lighter, the blow torch came to life. He fired the flame into the air and then positioned it within whispering distance of Baron's right ear. Baron instinctively moved his head, but Ronnie kept the flame close. Tony leaned forward.

'If you don't tell me what I need to know, my friend here is going to burn your ears off and if he does that you're not going to be able to hear what else I gotta say are you?'

Baron began breathing heavily as the heat from the flame became unbearable. His notoriety was being painfully melted away. Thoughts of being murdered and buried in some uninhabited woodland, felt all too real. He began to cough as the hot fumes scorched his throat.

'I think he wants to say something, Ron.'

Ronnie looked Baron in the face.

'Well?'

'Alright! Alright! Mi did tek duh drugs.'

Tony cupped his ear, as if he hadn't heard.

'You did what?'

'I took yuh drugs.'

Ronnie smiled a smile of satisfaction as he turned down the flame. He leaned over Baron.

'Who's a naughty boy?'

Angered, Tony gripped Baron by the throat.

'I want my stuff back, every last kilo. Do you hear me?'

Baron struggled to speak, until Tony released his hand.

'You were saying?'

'I said alright, I'll get back yuh drugs. Mi jus need some time.'

'Oh I know you will. This ain't Jamaica; you can't go around robbing and shooting people. There are repercussions for that type of behaviour. That brings me on to my second issue. Malik Simms.'

Baron looked up, surprised.

'A little bird tells me your son's bought a piece and is threatening to shoot my boy.'

'How yuh know Malik?'

'How do I know Malik? He works for me mate. He's a good kid, ain't he Ronnie?'

'Err, yeah mate.' Ronnie hesitated, trying to ignore the picture in his head.

Tony got right into Baron's face.

'I'm gonna keep it simple. If you or your son as much as breathe near him and if I don't get back what belongs to me, you're gonna find yourself flying back to Jamaica in a wooden box. Are we understood?'

Baron gave a submissive nod. His spirit was broken and on the floor. The pain soon returned to his knee, forcing him to close his eyes. Tony picked up the cloth hood and placed it back over Baron's head.

'Pull the van up Ron; we'll dump him near a hospital. His knee is hanging off, mate.'

It was pitch black and cold outside. He could see the light beaming from the entrance to the A & E department in the distance. Disorientated, he squeezed through some dense bushes towards the road. He had dragged his broken leg across what seemed like miles of woodland. Baron struggled to swallow the humiliation. The pain tested his threshold to its limits as he stumbled down a muddy bank onto a narrow pathway. He steadied himself, removed his sweatshirt and wrapped it tightly around his knee. He had no idea of the time or where he was. But he was sure that he was nowhere near London.

Front Page News

Knocking back neat vodka, Katherine opened her laptop, wincing as the alcohol bit the back of her throat. It was 9.30pm and the day had been less than fruitful. Scraping the bottom of the pot for enough morsels to make a decent story was not her idea of great journalism. She tied her hair up into a bun; exposing the faint freckles on her high cheekbones.

Managing the payments on her penthouse apartment was becoming increasingly difficult. Her father, a Labour MP had point blank refused to gift her with any golden nuggets from inside the walls of the House of Commons, stating that she would have to find her own way and her own stories.

Katherine pressed the play button on her iPod and put it in the docking station. She began to type as the classical music smoothed its way through the Bose speakers. Recent events were provoking her conscience; she looked up at a picture of her graduation on the wall as a sense of failure overtook her mind. Her thoughts began to drift away in a stream of self-pity. *I didn't study all those years to be some cheap corrupt journalist, did I? Dad must really think I'm a waste of space; if he ever knew I was in the pockets of those bloody police, he'd probably have a heart attack.*

DCS Rogers and DCI Wilkes's faces spun around her head. Her career was still in the starter block, waiting for a worthy headline to fire her into stardom. Baron was big news; he was the Lord of the dark side of Tottenham. He controlled the drugs coming in and out of the area. She was almost sure that if she followed the trail of recent murders she would probably end up at Baron's front door. But nobody had more inside information than Rogers and Wilkes. Neighbourhood groups had even protested outside the police station, wanting answers. They couldn't understand how drugs were being openly sold in full view of the public and nothing was being done.

Katherine downed another drink. Her inhibitions began to waver. The more she thought about Rogers and Wilkes, the more guilt she felt. She didn't know Nathan Lewis personally but putting him in prison for something he didn't do was not sitting well with her, it wasn't her style. Private school educated and from a wealthy family, she was taught to respect the law. But she was hell bent on proving to her father that she could make it without his financial backing.

She picked up her mobile phone from the sofa and then slid open the door to her balcony. As the fresh air caressed her face, a dizzy spell caused her to stumble forward almost dropping the bottle of vodka hanging loosely between her two fingers. Looking across the river from her Shad Thames apartment, she could see the London Eye slowly making its full circle. It reminded her of her career, moving slow, yet seemingly routed to the spot. Turning to her phone, she scrolled her address book through blurred eyes, unsure of what she was going to say.

'You have reached DCS Rogers, I am unable to take your call, please leave your name and number and I'll get back to you...'

'Rogers will you answer your phone? This is Katherine Peterson. I think it's time you give me a call. I've done my bit, now I want the Baron story. What's taking so long? Shouldn't he be in prison by now? Call me when you get this message or I might just write a story about dodgy police. Do you hear me? I'm waiting for your call.'

She turned back to the bottle. It was empty. Journalism was proving more of a challenge than she thought; it was exposing her vulnerability. A cold side that was susceptible to bribery. Examining the scar on her hand took her back to that rainy night, when they had robbed her. She was still unsure whether it was stupidity or lack of street smarts that had her fighting back. *Was it bloody worth it?* She looked back at her open laptop. *Should have let them take it. It's caused me nothing but trouble anyway.* Looking up at the sky, she wondered why she couldn't see a single star. Her phone interrupted her thoughts.

Dad Calling! She answered, more willingly than usual.

'Hello, old boy. How are you?'

'Old boy? Katherine, have you been drinking?'

'Drinking ... *me*? Nooo! I'm just happy to hear from you.'

'You sound very slurred to me.'

Katherine laughed.

'So, how are you and the rest of your old Labour farts?'

'Look, I think it might be best I call back another time. You're obviously drunk.'

'No, Dad ... wait.'

'What's wrong, Katherine?'

'I have a story. It could be big.'

'I hope it's nothing to do with these murdering little hoodies.'

Second thoughts entered her head. Her father had no attachment to life on a forgotten council estate. But she had grown empathetic after spending a year with the South London Press. She'd covered a spate of stabbings and seen some extreme levels of dysfunction.

She paused, aware that the drink was liberating her.

'Dad, what would you say if I told you that two highly ranked police officers were colluding with a drug dealer?'

'What are you talking about? How much have you had to drink?'

Katherine sighed.

'As usual, you don't want to listen to me. I've got a story and it's only a matter of time before it's all over the papers.'

'What officers? You don't do dirt on your own, your Uncle spent 25 years in the force, you should be proud. Anyway, these drug dealers serve a purpose.'

'Dad, what are you saying?'

'Why do you care about what happens in these urban ghettos? I didn't join politics to concern myself with such matters. You start accusing the police, you could compromise my position... just leave it alone.'

Katherine's emotions began to churn as a single tear ran down her cheek onto her blouse.

'Dad, I am 28 years old and you're still dictating to me. I've seen a different side of life and I'm not ...' her voice broke. 'I'm just not sure what is right or wrong anymore. I need a story, something that would get on the front pages. Not some four-line column in some bloody local paper. You obviously don't care about my career.'

She heard a long sigh.

'You go ahead and cut your own throat, just don't have mine cut in the process. And in case you haven't noticed, proving a case against the police is virtually impossible. They look after their own.'

'Well that depends doesn't it. You always taught me to keep my trump card close to my chest. Her spinning head was now full of probabilities and possibilities.

'Bye Dad.'

She hung up and then the phone immediately began screaming, Rogers calling!

'Hello!'

'Miss Peterson, I just listened to your message. Very interesting. We had a deal, did we not?'

'Well yes and I've been very patient. So what's happening?'

'Look luv, Baron is big news. Not just here, in Jamaica as well. These things take time. I've got informants working on the ground. Just found out that he sacrifices a few drugs mules to keep us off the scent, when in fact he is shipping tons of cocaine through his cash and carry business. As I said before, we can make a lot of money off this; then we'll pull the plug. You're not going to win with a story based on speculation ... besides you dropped his son in it. So don't throw your toys out the pram now.'

Katherine stepped back out onto the balcony, she felt hot.

'I didn't sign up to this. I want out.'

'Too late luv, you're already in. What would your father say if he knew that you framed a kid for a story...aye? Daughter of Labour MP, Tim Peterson in the frame. Now there's a front page story.'

A party boat cruised along the river, taking Katherine's mind briefly off the conversation. She wished she was on it.

Bangers and Cash

❖

Malik stepped out of the rain, removing his wet jacket. The garage was unusually quiet, with only two cars sitting on the ramps.

Tony looked up at the dusty wall clock, shaking his head. You're on time. What, you wet the bed or summink?'

Nodding, Malik hung up his jacket.

'Nah Boss, I'm just trying to move differently ... be on time and dat.'

Tony smiled.

'Good idea. Anyway, good to have you back. A few things have changed since you were last here. Well, Zoe ain't here for starters.'

Malik stopped in his tracks.

'Where is she, Boss?'

'Her old man sent her to Spain to look after one of his nightclubs out there. I tell you, you're lucky he didn't kill you. What were you thinking?'

Malik looked down at the oil-stained floor. He felt guilty, yet a part of him missed her. Just for a moment, she made him feel safe. She was

different— white and rich. Not his usual type, but she had the life he craved. He breathed in, briefly remembering the smell of her perfume. Tony watched intently.

'Oi! Snap out of it! She's gone, mate.'

'Nah, I'm good Boss'

Tony pointed across the garage.

'Whatever you say, son. Grab a spanner and take the back box off that A6.'

'I got it, Boss.'

'And stop calling me *Boss*.'

Malik half grinned as he slipped into his overalls. The garage phone rang, taking Tony's attention away from Malik. 'This better not be one of those salespeople from India ... getting on my last nerve.'

Tony bowled across the workshop and grabbed the phone off the workbench.

'Before you say anything, yes I am happy with my mobile phone, my gas supplier, electric supplier, car insurance and — come to think of it — I'm happy with my wife as well.'

There was a long silence at the other end of the line.

'...Hello.'

'What you on about, Chaucer? It's Ronnie, you plonker.'

Tony chuckled.

'Sorry mate. I've been getting those bloody calls. You know, people trying to sell you summink—'

Ronnie interrupted.

'Come to think of it, I am a kind of salesman. Just not the kind of goods you'd wanna sell to your mother.' He laughed at his own humour.

Tony jammed the phone between his ear and his shoulder and began digging grease from his finger nails.

'So, to what do I owe this call?'

'Listen mate, I got a job for your boy.'

'Who, Malik?'

'Yeah mate. I think you owe me one; one for not breaking his neck and one for dealing with that Jamaican twat.'

'What's this job then? Hope it's nothing too heavy.'

'Nah mate...just a small one, and there's a couple grand in it for him and more work if he pulls it off.'

Tony looked over at Malik, lowering his voice.

'What's the details?'

'You remember that old Ford Fiesta the missus used to drive — the old rust bucket that was in the back of my garage?'

'Yeah I remember. That's what she was driving when you first met - anyway, what about it?'

'She's only gone and had a garage clear-out while I was out in Spain; sold the car to some dodgy car dealer. He told her some crap about it being a classic and he wants to do it up.

Tony frowned.

'What's your point?'

'Well Tone, my point is, I had bloody twenty large hidden under the spare tyre.'

'Twenty grand?'

'Yeah mate. She doesn't know about it and I need it back.'

'So why don't you just go down there and get it?'

'Well that's the problem; the old bill is all over me. Remember that geezer they found in the Thames a few years back? They think I had summink to do with it ... reckon they got a witness. I gotta keep my nose clean and ride this one out.'

'So where's Malik come in to it.'

Ronnie paused.

'He can handle himself, right?'

'Yeah mate, he can chuck it about a bit.'

'Well to be honest, I need him to go down the car lot — the one on Acre Street.'

'What? Don't that belong to Trevor O'Brien's lot?

'Yeah, but their cousin Lee runs it now ... city boy.'

'Ok, so you want Malik to go down there and bosh him up a bit and get your money back.

'That lot, they ain't gonna let someone just go digging around in the back of the car. They only understand violence. I'm hoping the money is still in there. He just needs to get the keys, grab the dosh and get out of there...they won't know it come from me.'

Tony sighed heavily.

'Ok, suppose I owe you one — just leave it with me. I'm supposed to be keeping this kid out of trouble.'

Baron sat flicking his cigarette lighter. A half-moon had just made an appearance between some high-rise flats in the distance. Apart from some movement coming from a nearby houseboat, the night was still and bitterly cold. He watched the gentle flow of the River Lea under the moonlight and mentally totted up some figures. Things needed tidying up before a risky trip to Jamaica.

'Money is everyting,' he whispered under his breath, justifying his lifestyle.

The sound of tyres coasting across the gravel car park took his attention away from his increasing stash of money. Counting down the seconds, he waited for the car to pull up. Voices crackled through a police radio, confirming the arrival of Matthews and Thompson. Baron reached into the passenger seat for his walking stick, before getting out of the car.

Thompson emerged from a dark BMW, followed by Matthews, who was preoccupied on the phone. Thompson extended his hand towards Baron, who kept his in his hand at his side.

'Mr Lewis ... you showed up this time. What's with the walking stick ... someone done your kneecaps?'

Baron laughed, embarrassed

'No worry yuhself, just ah football ting.'

Matthews eyed him suspiciously as he ended his phone call.

'So is that why you didn't show up last Tuesday

then? We can't be sitting around here with a carload of drugs ... might get pulled by the police.'

Thompson laughed, amused by his colleagues sarcasm.

Baron kissed his teeth.

'You must tek me fi puppy show ... bout police. Di two ah you are *bomba* police.'

Thompson handed over a black holdall.

'Learn to take a joke, mate.'

Baron eyed the contents of the bag.

'Dis look light, where di rest deh.'

Matthew's grinned indiscriminately.

'Well I had to sample the goods, didn't I, make sure it's good stuff.'

Baron eyed Matthews.

'You ah tek liberties ... mi garn yeah.'

Thompson walked back to his car and then turned back towards Baron.

'Same place, 8.00 - in a month's time.'

Malik pulled the balaclava over his head and glanced at Stuart, who was busy removing his glasses.

'Rah, geek to bad man in five seconds. Yuh look mad different without the glasses blud.'

Stuart half-grinned.

'Yeah mate, nuff man try rob me and get banged up. Man, don't know I got pure Irish travellers' blood in me. Yuh get me, fam.'

Malik could feel the coldness in his green eyes. Since Tubbs's death, they had got close, despite their different backgrounds. Stuart's parents had fled violence in Northern Ireland and settled in Hackney with Stuart's grandfather, who had lived in the area since his late teens. He had often told Stuart stories about the discrimination he'd faced and how he'd fought side by side with the black fellas. Stuart was just one of a handful of white boys at his secondary school, but he had held his own. Malik admired his split personalities and his fearless spirit.

A silver Mercedes C Class pulled up at the gate to the car lot. Malik and Stuart were crouched between two shipping containers. Malik looked out as the car door opened and a slim blonde haired man stepped out from the vehicle.

'Dis looks like the boss man, blud.'

Stuart nodded in agreement.

The man, who looked to be in his late thirties, fixed his white shirt into his trousers and adjusted his tie before fiddling with a bunch of keys. Surveying the car lot, he opened the padlocked gate and then got back into his car.

Malik adjusted his face mask and then squeezed his hands into his black leather gloves.

'Dis one's for Tubbs, yeah,' he whispered under his breath, feeling a surge of guilt over his deceased friend.

Stuart removed a steel baseball bat from a sports holdall and put on his own gloves. A private jet passed overhead, heading for city airport. Malik observed the aircraft as it disappeared eastward. His mind filled with presumptuous thoughts of working for Ronnie on a level that could potentially bring him bundles of money. A nudge from Stuart interrupted his daydream, bringing him back to earth.

'You can't afford one a dem, fam.'

Malik paused to straighten his thinking.

'I'm aiming big blud. Dis is jus the starters.'

Stuart held out his fist, which Malik touched with his own.

'Let's do this ting!'

They hustled their way into the car lot and headed towards a grey Portakabin, which served as the sales office.

Once at the door, Malik put a finger to his lips. 'Shhhhh!'

He grasped the door handle and pushed it open.

Stuart rushed into the office, startling the man up from his desk.

Stuart pushed the bat into his face.

'Where yuh going, mate?'

Shaken, the man gazed into Stuart's eyes unaware of Malik.

'Da – da — do you know who dis gaff belongs to mate? You're — you're a dead man.'

Stuttering, he tried to turn the tables, but Malik

wasn't there for a conversation.

Malik shoved Stuart to one side and gripped the man by the collar.

'Shut up, blud. I don't care who dis place belongs to.'

'What, you black—'

Before he could finish his sentence Malik released a lethal head-butt, knocking his head back against a large framed picture. Malik pulled Stuart out the way as the man stumbled sideways into a drinks machine and then fell to the floor almost in slow motion.

Blood spattered his fresh white shirt and dripped onto the carpet. He clambered back to his feet, using the desk for leverage. Holding his nose together, he looked up.

'What do you want lads? There ain't any money here.'

'Keys to the Ford Fiesta. No long ting?'

Malik demanded.

Confused, the man clumsily opened the top desk drawer.

'What do you want that old banger for, it don't even run?'

Malik became impatient.

'Jus pass duh keys. Don't let my boy have to break the bat roun yuh head.'

'Alright, alright. Hold on, the keys are here.'

He passed Stuart a single key with a paper tag.

Malik took the key from Stuart and then turned

towards the door.

'Keep him there and buss his head if yuh ave to. I'm gonna get duh ting.'

Stuart nodded.

'I got dis, fam.'

Once out in the yard, Malik scanned through the rows of cars for the red Fiesta. His heart began to race; he could almost smell the raw money. He dodged in and out of the vehicles but still couldn't see the old car.

A wrenching thought entered his head. He saw Zoe, then Ronnie's icy stare freezing him to the spot. *Dis might be a setup, blud. Nah, can't be, Tony wouldn't let my man have me up like dis.* He stood still for a moment. *I don't think dis car is even here ... nah bun dat.*

He headed back towards the Portakabin, still scanning the small plot of land. On the verge of giving up, he spotted a small workshop just behind an old caravan. At the front, he could just make out a small vehicle covered over in a grey tarpaulin. He ran over, peering through the office window as he passed. Stuart was in control, like he knew he would be.

It began to rain, it had been threatening to all morning. Malik lifted the covering to reveal a red bonnet and mentally matched the number plate against the one in his head. It matched. Running round to the back, he quickly opened the bonnet and lifted out the spare tyre.

'Rah, can't believe it.'

A square-shaped bag wrapped in brown tape sat at the base of the car. Malik grabbed the package and texted Stuart:

'Got it'.

He moved swiftly through the gate, removing his balaclava. A maroon Range Rover cruised past him and entered the yard. Panicked, Malik turned and could see Stuart running towards the entrance. The car door swung open and two large men edged out as Stuart approached. The driver stuck out a foot and sent Stuart hurtling to the ground.

Malik stopped and shouted back.

'Get up, blud. *Run!*'

Stuart was back on his feet in seconds as the man began to bear down on him. He quickly retrieved the baseball bat, which had rolled under the vehicle and swung, missing the man and breaking the passenger window.

Malik stood back watching. He could hear shouting.

Stuart dodged a sluggish punch from the big fella and slammed the bat into his ribs, sending him sideways.

Before his accomplice could get to him, Stuart broke into a sprint and caught up with Malik who was already standing by Stuart's Vauxhall Astra. He pulled out his keys and hit the central locking button.

He looked back to the car lot and could see the two men getting into the Range Rover. Once in the car, Stuart started the engine, slammed the gear into reverse and backed out onto the side street. He then pushed it into first gear and floored the accelerator, wheel spinning the car over the wet tarmac.

After joining the dual carriageway, he moved into the outside lane and gave the SRi engine some juice.

Malik scanned out the back window.

'Put the back wiper on ... I can't see.'

Stuart flicked the switch and checked the rear-view mirror.

'Can yuh see dem?'

Malik looked back as far as his vision would allow.

'Nah blud, we lost dem,' He laughed.

Stuart laughed with him.

'Back to Hackney, blud.'

Evil Mist

Whoever it was, they were annoyingly persistent. The doorbell rang for the fourth time, prompting Claudette to draw back the curtain. As she looked down from the bay window, she recognised Baron's Lexus parked across the road.

Baron shouted up from the front garden,

'Open di door nah ...'

Claudette fixed her dressing gown and ambled downstairs. She picked up the mail from the doormat and released the security chain before opening the door.

'What's your problem, ringing off my doorbell?'

'Where Nathan deh?'

'Hello to you too ...he's in bed. What's going on?'

'Mi need fi talk to him.'

Claudette stepped out of Baron's way, avoiding his walking stick.

'What happened to your leg?'

Baron kissed his teeth.

'Everybody waan know bout mi leg ... cha.' He hobbled up the stairs and disappeared down the corridor.

Claudette sighed as she shuffled through the letters. Other than EastEnders and Holby City, she didn't need any more drama in her life. But Baron was a drama, a movie and the sequel rolled into one. Since meeting him at a family wedding, she had ridden a psychological rollercoaster that had nearly spat her out at a mental health institution.

Gunshots through her window, attempted kidnaps, police raids — she had gone through it and come out the other side with a twenty year old son and a semi-detached house on the outskirts of Enfield to show for it.

She split from Baron when Nathan was around 10 years old and had religiously tried to limit Baron's access to him. But the damage had already been done; he'd already been exposed to extreme violence and to multiple men who never became part of the furniture.

Teachers couldn't deal with the angry black boy. He looked disturbed and beyond help. After another erratic outburst he was excluded then transferred to a Pupil Referral Unit. It took less than six weeks for the head teacher to throw in the towel. She felt that she had a duty to protect the other boys who were angels compared to Nathan. He soon ended up on the street, robbing schoolboys at first, then selling weed on a small scale. After being robbed by members of the Milly Boys, he began recruiting his own foot soldiers and formed D.O.A. (Dead on Arrival). He had a twisted desire to make it the wickedest and most violent gang in London, adopting the name 'Ninja' after he stabbed two youths in a party and jumped from a second floor balcony.

A visit from Baron always churned up bad memories, memories Claudette wanted to pack away and bury for good. She looked upstairs and made as if to go up, but then opted to go into the kitchen to put the kettle on.

Baron entered his son's room.

'Nathan, wake up nuh man.'

A deep grumble rolled beneath the covers, but no movement. Baron walked over to the window and opened it as wide as it would go, letting in a winter breeze.

'Cha, Mum! What yuh opening duh window for?' Nathan emerged from the duvet, his eyes were glazed over and fiery red.

'Rah Dad ... wha gwaan? When did you get here?'

'Mi jus reach. Mi haf fi talk to you.'

Nathan sat up and rested his head against a poster of Scarface just above his bed. Baron hung his stick on the door handle and sat down on the end of the bed.

'Remember mi tell yuh not fi go trouble dis Malik bwoy ... well mi inna pure problem right now. Dem Babylon ah mess wid mi food. Dem waan tek ah bigger cut and plus mi owe Tony ah whole heap ah drugs...'

Nathan raised an eyebrow.

'What do yuh mean Dad? Who's Tony?'

'Long story. Mi cyaan talk bout dat right now. Mi looking fi forward to Jamaica tonight. Mi nah come back yah fi a while ... mi had to pay off one Police sergeant over deh fi put mi murder charge pon ah next man, so mi can come een.'

Nathan listened intently. 'What murder?'

'Son, yuh Dad has done sum wicked tings ... but ah so it go. Darg eat darg.' He paused, stroking his goatee beard.

'So I was saying, if yuh feel say dis bwoy disrespeck you, then go deal wid him. After today, mi gaan ... tings ah get too hot inna London right now.'

He reached into his coat pocket and produced some folded paperwork. He separated two tickets and then passed one to Nathan.

'When yuh dun, fly out to Jamaica. Come meet mi. Dem nah find you out deh ... mi know sum proper Rasta man who can look after you until tings calm down. Yuh get mi. Den we link up lickle more.'

Nathan remained in a stunned silence. The revelation was heavy, but in a strange way, refreshing. He was struggling to contain his hatred of Malik. He wanted him dead, plain and simple. But now he had a viable way of escape, although he had no real desire to live in Jamaica. He thought he could hop from there over to the US, where he had cousins.

He read the date on the ticket.

'What about mum? Dis only gives me two weeks.'

'Look, after a few years yuh can come back ah

London.'

Baron got up and held out his fist to touch Nathan's.

Nathan looked into his father's eyes. They were emotionless. Deep down he yearned for an embrace, a strong hug, but his father didn't seem to know how to. He touched fists with him.

Baron removed his walking stick from the door handle.

'Mi will pass and check yuh, when mi ah go ah airport.'

'Ok dad, cool. Later.'

The door closed. Nathan looked up at the dusty suitcase perched above his wardrobe.

Dis is deep ... Jamaica. He got up and glanced across the road through the window. A magpie landed on the window ledge, startling him. It peered through the glass and then flew off again. 'Rah ... dat was weird, blud.' Shaking his head, he walked over to his bedside cabinet and slid a screwdriver out from under a pile of magazines. He pulled his bed away from the wall and squeezed into the gap. He prised up one of the floorboards and removed a cloth wrap, checking over his shoulder before sitting back on the bed. Slowly he unravelled the fabric, grinning sadistically as depraved thoughts played through his mind. *My man's getting duppied...I swear down.*

He lusted over the gun with his finger tucked behind the trigger. Hearing his mother's footsteps coming up the stairs, he quickly discarded the weapon, pushed the bed back into position and mentally prepared for an interrogation about his father. She had no idea that he had bonded with him in the worst possible way.

Malik finished counting the cash and put it into a plastic bag, keeping a mental note of the four grand. The money was coming fast. A few more favours for Ronnie would set him up nicely. It was risky, but it was paying. He felt a sense of heaviness on his chest. A strange feeling, it was like fear but somehow different. Pushing the money under the mattress, he began to think about recent events. He cradled his head in his hands and tried to make sense of it all. *Dis is a madness...man can't even relax in his own yard yuh know.* Glancing around the room he began to wonder whether his mother would ever get them away from the bleakness of the estate. He weighed up his options. *I can stay here, work for Ronnie and dodge Ninja a little longer, or just take the money and move out duh endz. It's like man'z trying to torture me wid sum psychological warfare. What's he on? He wants to try move to me an ketch me slipping. I know how he thinks ... Ninja's ah madman.* Malik got up and began to pace the room. He felt strange inside; a warm sensation filled his stomach but it didn't feel nice. It felt intrusive and somewhat oppressive. Frustrated, he punched the wardrobe door. *Nah blud... something don't feel right.* His BlackBerry began vibrating, making his heart jump.

'Sticky, wha gwaan?'
'Murkz, hear what. My girl just called me and said Ninja is coming for you tonight blud.'
Malik tensed as coldness ran down his back.
'Wot ... yuh sure?'
'Yeah fam, she's one of dem D.O.A. man'z sister.
'Duh same girl I done a ting wid.'
Malik paused, reflecting.
'Sticky, how come you keep giving me info all of a sudden. In fact, I didn't ketch up with you about the time you were supposed to bring duh mopeds.'
'Yeah I know.'
'Yuh know what? All I know is you didn't turn up and D.O.A. ran up in my yard and try kill me.'
'Listen Murkz, last summer I tried to check your girl in duh park. I didn't know she was your girl until Roman told me, innit. She kinda dissed me, so I was vexed. So I told dem man where you lived.'
'Wot? Are you mad, fam?
'It was a mistake man.'
Malik punched the wardrobe for a second time.
Sticky heard the bang, but didn't comment.
'So, what, dis is your way of smoothing tings over wid me. Trying ta save yuh neck and dat ... don't want man to come bang you up.'
'I owe you big time, I know. Roman told me how

you roll, blud.'

'Yeah yuh owe big time, fi real. Yuh gonna have ta earn yuh stripes roun here. I coulda dead cos of you and yuh try check my girl as well...are you mad, fam?'

'I owe you ... I owe you, yeah.' Sticky sounded panicked.

Malik cut the phone call and then called Lenny. The phone rang several times and then went to voicemail.

'Len, it's Murkz — I mean Malik. Call me ASAP.'

He rested the phone down on top of the bible, which was still opened on Psalms 31 V 13. Since the day his mother had asked him to read it, he'd left it open, half believing that maybe God would protect him. He pondered for a moment and then read the scripture again. Looking up at the ceiling, he thought about praying but didn't know how. He remembered his mother used to tell him that he could just talk to God. Lowering his head, he crouched down on one knee and squeezed his eyes shut.

'Erm God, I ain't really spoken to you before...but right now, man'z in trouble —'

His BlackBerry began vibrating, throwing him off course. It was Lenny.

'Len, thanks for calling man.'

'Malik, what's wrong?'

'Ninja's coming for me tonight. Some yout jus baited him up.'

'What ... nah he can't be. I sorted that out.'

'What do yuh mean you sorted it out? Len talk to me.'

There was a long pause.

'Tony done me a favour and warned him off.'

'What ... fi real. Like how?'

'He didn't tell me how. All I know is he went via Nathan's dad.'

'Who, Baron? Nooo! Why did you get involved like dat?'

'I tried to help you man. Baron is the only person Nathan will listen to ... the boy worships his dad. Trust me.'

Malik rubbed his head.

'So how come I'm hearing he's coming for me den?'

'Who told you that?'

'One yunga called Sticky ... I don't know his real name.'

Lenny thought for a few seconds.

'Oh that little teef- loves teefing mopeds.'

'Yeah, dat's him. He rolls wid duh Milly Boys,'

Lenny chuckled, not amused.

'Yeah and he ain't been in Hackney long. Boy's probably trying to get his little reputation up. Probably wants to use your name for back-up. Malik, I don't think you realise how much weight your name carries. I hear a lot of youts talking about how Murkz banged up four D.O.A. man.

'What...fi real?'

Lenny laughed in an attempt to lighten the mood.

'Malik, Murkz has superseded you.'

'Len, I respect you man. But I ain't too sure about dis. I've been getting some weird feeling from dis morning. Dat was even before Sticky called me. It's like something was just hovering around me.'

'Do you want me to call Tony?'

'Nah man. I need to duck out duh endz. Can you help me wid dat? I got money.'

'Hold on, let me think.'

Lenny ran through the directory in his head.

'Wait ... I got an idea. My younger brother Bradley lives in Chatham. I can arrange for you to go down there. Only thing is, he ain't got space at the moment. But you could stay in a B & B near his flat until we can sort something more long term.'

'Where's dat? Chatham, I ain't heard of it.'

'It's in Kent, out the way.'

'Yeah man...dat sounds alright still. I need to be gone by dis afternoon.'

The 16.04 train to Chatham pulled into platform 5. Victoria Station was at its usual crowded capacity. Malik bit into his Snickers bar and hoisted his holdall onto his shoulder. As the doors opened, he stepped into what felt like another dimension; a dimension that was going to beam him from an urban prison to the unknown. He found a seat next to the window and sat down. After withstanding a few dubious looks, he huddled down for the ride.

The train soon eased away from the platform. Already he was feeling a few pounds lighter than when he left his Hackney estate. His burdens began to dissipate as the train gathered speed. Looking out across the tracks, he studied the periodic graffiti jotted around on derelict buildings and walls. He thought of his younger days, when he used to carry a black marker pen wherever he went and tag his name wherever possible.

The train passed over a busy high street. Malik observed the scores of people busy in their own worlds. He wondered what it would be like in Kent; he'd only had brief encounters with the countryside, thanks to Tony and Zoe. But it was enough for him to consider a possible move away from London and the environment that often felt like a warzone. Kia had often spoken about living in the sticks, but at the time he couldn't see her vision.

His phone began vibrating in his pocket, jumping him from his thoughts.

'Babe, what's up?'

'Where are you?'

Malik hesitated.

'...Erm, I'm on a train to Kent.'

'Kent? I don't get it ... what you going there for?'

'Babe it's long. Ninja's on me.'

'Yeah, but he's always been on you.'

'Nah it's different dis time ... he's got a strap.

Man'z looking to take me out.'

Kia went quiet; Malik could almost feel her heart pounding down the phone line.

'Why you didn't tell me? I don't understand ...'

Her voice began to shake.

'...who's in Kent? When are you coming back?'

Malik knew that tears were probably flowing down her face. He tried to swallow the guilt, but this time he couldn't, she'd touched a place in his usually stony heart.

'I'm not sure ... I'm going to check it out down there. If I like it, then maybe we can move out duh endz. I mean dat's wot you want innit.'

Kia sniffled.

'Yeah I do...you know I do. I just want you, me and Daniel. I want a bit of peace without worrying about you every minute. I don't wanna raise Daniel round here.'

Malik sighed, it all sounded like some fairy tale but deep down; he wanted it to be real. In that brief moment that he'd spent with Zoe in front of the fireplace, he'd realised that there was more to the life that he was currently living.

'Babe, I'm gonna try and make it happen...but we need money and I only know one way of making proper peas.'

Kia went quiet; he had an idea what she was thinking. He could hear intruding pauses coming from her line.

Kia broke her silence.

'Hold on babe, I got a call coming through.'

Malik pulled his hood over his head, partly because the old lady in the adjacent seat was listening to his phone call and partly because he felt like sleeping. He waited for Kia to come back on the line.

Lenny lowered the driver window and stared down the long line of cars. There seemed to be more going on than the usual Friday evening rush. He checked the time on the dashboard: 6.30pm. Police sirens echoed in the distance and gradually got louder. Malik was on his mind, but he was relieved that he was out of harm's way. He guessed he was probably settling into the B&B. He thought about calling him but then lost his patience. After some tight manoeuvres, he spun the Audi out of the traffic and performed a smooth three point turn. He then gunned back up the Lower Clapton Road before swinging left into the first available side road. Putting his foot down, he quickly shifted through the gears. He wanted to check in on a boy he was helping with some bullying issues before taking Marcia out to dinner. It was their 10th wedding anniversary and he'd booked a table at their favourite Nepalese restaurant.

Turning right at the end of the road, he then drove along a small common. On the other side of the green he noticed reams of flashing blue lights and lots of people milling around. Slowing down, he studied the scene with one eye still on the road. It was just a few yards in front of the alleyway, close to Kia's estate. He sighed, shaking his head with a grave thought already firmly imprinted in his mind. It was a scene he'd visited one time too many.

He mumbled about the traffic under his breath, still looking at the activities unfolding. He could see cars backing up further down the road. Reluctantly he found a parking spot and stepped out of the car. He felt a sense of duty to find out what was going on.

The police would be knocking his door anyway, they always did. They used him as a mediator, but a lot of the time he felt that they were just ticking boxes to keep the residents happy. Lenny took a slow jog across the damp grass. As he got closer, he could see an ambulance, paramedics and several representatives from the police fraternity who were taping off the area.

He approached a group of youths, who were sitting on bikes, talking excitedly as if they had just watched a movie at the Odeon.

'You lot, what's happening?'

A youth broke from the bunch and rode up to Lenny. It was Roman.

'Lenny...it's a madness.'

'What's happened, man?'

'Somebody's duppied Ninja. He's dead, blud.'

Lenny's eyebrows curved inwards with anxiety.

'What, you sure?'

'Course I'm sure ... somebody shot him. He was dead before duh paramedics even reached.'

'What ... fi real?'

'Yeah man, I got shook; I thought it was Murkz lying there. Then I see dem covering duh body innit. Blatantly Ninja ... boy looks evil even when he's dead.'

Lenny looked over at the dreaded picture and then back at Roman.

'Nah, Malik ain't around man. Thank God. Do you know what happened?'

Roman pointed to a woman in a long padded coat.

'Dat woman there...I think she's Kia's mum. She heard some argument going on at the side of the block. Next ting she said she heard a gunshot go off... by duh time she came down, she just found Ninja bleeding out all over duh place. Most people stayed in the block, they were too frightened to come out, yuh get me.'

Lenny looked up to the sky, his heart wrenched inside. Ninja's death could possibly unearth the living hell. He turned back to Roman.

'Do you know who done it?

Roman shook his head.

'Nah blud. Could be anybody. Ninja had nuff enemies.'

Lenny thought for a moment.
'Where's that yout ... Sticky?'
Roman shrugged his shoulders.
'I ain't seen him today.'
'Ok, thanks ... we'll catch up soon.'
Lenny's date with his wife had all but disappeared from his mind as he strolled over to talk to the police.

The Garden of England

❖

He handed the cab driver the piece of paper and sunk into the back seat. The cabbie read it and then started the engine.

'Maidstone Road, mate — it's just up the road. You look like a fit lad, you could have walked it.'

'Nah ... I've just travelled down from London. I don't know round these sides.'

'Yeah, I used to live in London...Peckham mate.'

'Wot? Dat place is grimy.'

'Yeah, it has got a bit dirty since I left.'

'Nah, I don't mean dirty — oh don't worry about it man. It's long.'

The cabbie chuckled.

'I ain't got a clue what you're on about mate. Anyway, that B&B is just up here on the left. Olive House you wanted, yeah.'

Malik looked out of the window.

'I don't know Boss, you've got duh piece of paper.'

'Olive House B&B...there you go mate. Just call it a fiver.'

Malik took a wad of money out from his back pocket and peeled off a ten pound note, before handing it to the driver.

'Keep duh change, Boss.'

'Enjoy your stay. I wouldn't go back to Peckham

if you promised me a pint of beer and a fit blonde, mate.'

Malik half laughed and turned towards the green front door of a large Victorian house. A security light beamed into his face as he stepped up onto a quaint porch. *Olive House B&B.* He read the wooden plaque which was secured to the brickwork just to the right of a hanging flower basket.

Hesitant, he tapped the brass knocker against the door and waited. After a few seconds, he could hear footsteps. He took a couple of steps back until the door opened. A grey haired woman of retirement age stood in the doorway looking Malik up and down as if he'd just fallen out of the sky.

'Yesss, can I help you?'

'I'm Malik, Malik Simms.'

The lady's expression remained blank, as if he was speaking Mongolian. He swung his bag from side to side, embarrassed.

'Lenny Grant ... uh ... he booked duh room for me.'

'Oh yes, Mr Grant...I don't know why you didn't say so in the first place. Come in young man.'

She opened the door wide.

'Follow me please.'

Halfway up the stairs, she turned and offered her hand.

'How rude of me — I'm Cynthia. And you are? I didn't catch your name.'

Malik shook her hand.

'Malik ... I came down from London.'

'Yes I know dear. Your friend told me all about you ... it just slipped my mind.'

She turned right at the top of the stairs and guided him to a door at the end of a long corridor.

'There you go: Room 4. The key is in the door. Lock it before you leave every morning. There's a key for the front door on there, but please ... not too late. Just use your discretion.'

Malik opened the door.

'Thanks a lot. Erm ... what time's breakfast?'

'Eight thirty.

Just join us in the dining room.'

'Thanks.'

Once in the room, he glanced around the amenities. It was a lot bigger and more inviting than his bedroom back in Hackney. The walls were painted in an earthy coffee brown with contrasting floral wallpaper on the wall behind the bed. A small flat screen TV jutted out above an antique dresser inside an alcove.

Wiping his brow, he sighed, relieved that he'd reached his destination. He suddenly remembered that his phone had died on the journey. After rummaging among the few belongs he'd managed to cram into the holdall, he located his charger and plugged it in. While the phone surged to life, he walked over to a small sink in the corner of the room and ran the cold tap. He splashed cold water on his face, hoping it would wash the dull pressure that was insistently building at his temples. Although he felt safe, he knew it would take a while to adjust to the new environment.

The BlackBerry came to life and immediately began pinging, followed by a stream of message alerts. He remembered the last time his phone had blown up in such a manner was on the day of the riots. Picking it up, he sat on the bed and read the first message:

Roman 'Millyboy Don': *Murkz holla at me... Ninja's dead.*

He froze, his hand began to shake. He read on:

Devil Boy: *Somebody got duppied...Ninjaaa looool*

Yunga Milly: *D.O. A. ...talk about karma.*

'Noooooo!' Malik threw the phone down. He began rocking back and forth, his eyes fixed on the wood floor.

'Nathan's dead,'

he muttered under his breath.

He'd unconsciously reverted to Ninja's birth name. The street connection had lost its relevance. He could only vision the skinny black boy he'd first met in Year 7. Kicking off his trainers, he fell back on the bed and put the pillow over his head.

Deciding to skip breakfast, Malik opted to read the book Lenny had given him. He'd read a chapter a while back and found every excuse since then not to get his head back into it. Even though the few pages he had read resonated with him, it was easier to stay ignorant.

Not wanting to dwell on events that were now out of his control, he decided to stay busy and enjoy whatever Kent had to offer in the way of distractions. Lenny's brother, Bradley, had scheduled to meet him down at the local lake. After a sneaky smoke from the bedroom window, he blasted his Lynx body spray to mask the odour. He grabbed the book and then headed downstairs to the kitchen.

'Good morning, young man. Had a goodnight's rest?'

'Yeah. I kinda passed out.'

'Yes, you did look a bit flustered when you arrived last night.'

Malik decided not to say too much. He wanted fresh air more than breakfast.

'Erm ... do you know where Capstone Lake is?'

'Yes I do. Have some breakfast first and I'll show you.'

'No thanks, I'm gonna skip the breakfast for today. I just need to get out.'

Cynthia turned over the bacon and then wiped

her hands on a tea towel.

'I've just done all this lovely bacon ... ok, suit yourself.'

A gentleman at the table cleared his throat and then interrupted.

'Excuse me but did I hear you say you want to go to the lake?'

Malik looked at Cynthia and then at the man.

'Err — yeah. Do yuh know where it is?'

'It's your lucky day. I'm heading to the golf course. I normally drive past the lake on the way. I'll give you a lift if you want.'

'You sure?'

'Of course I'm sure. I got to do my Samaritan bit for the day.'

'Cool...thanks for dat.'

Finishing his tea, the man got up from the table.

'That was a lovely breakfast as usual.'

Cynthia smiled, half embarrassed.

'Oh Tom, come on, the young man's waiting.'

'Ok, I'll see you later. I'm going to the church this evening for the youth meeting, so I'll be back quite late.

Cynthia strolled over to a second table, where a small family had just sat down for breakfast. She half turned her head.

'Okay, I'll see you then.'

Malik followed Tom out to the driveway. The air was brisk, but the sky showed signs of bringing a warm afternoon. Tom opened his boot and checked over his golf clubs and then waved at Malik to get into the car. He got in himself and stretched his arm across to Malik to shake his hand.

'So I guess you got my name ...Tom. And you are ...?'

Malik shook Tom's tight grip.

'I'm Malik.'

'It's nice to meet you, Malik.'

Tom turned out of the drive and headed East down the hill. Malik fiddled with his book. His head felt like his childhood toy box; filled to the brim with clutter.

'What's the book about?' Malik looked at Tom and quickly sized him up.

'Oh, you wouldn't really get it.'

'What, because I'm a middle class white man from Birmingham who drives a clapped out old Volvo?'

Malik searched for a reply.

'I didn't even know you were from Birmingham. I was just saying, duh book's got poetry and stuff about road life and dat.'

Tom smiled to himself, which angered Malik.

'Wot, is something funny?'

'I'm not laughing, young man. I'm just amused by the way you casually judged my whole character.'

Malik shrugged.

'Yeah well, I see what I see, innit.'

Tom reached onto the dashboard and handed

Malik a business card.

'Call me if you need to talk.'

Malik read the card: Pastor Tom Newland — *Gang Intervention Worker.*

'Rah, I had no clue, but why you giving dis to me?'

Tom took a sharp right turn onto a gravel pathway, then coasted for 20 yards. After turning into a gap in the trees, he stopped the car.

'The reason I've given you that card is because you are going to need it, but you just don't know it yet.'

Malik slipped the card into his book, thinking it would make an excellent bookmark.

'You don't know me.' His voice was raised.

'You don't know nuthin about me. Where's duh lake? I need to go.'

Tom dismissed Malik's rant and calmly pointed to a pathway between some overgrown bushes.

'The lake's through there.'

Malik slipped out of the car. 'Thanks ... appreciated the lift, still.'

Tom calmly smiled; he had a welcoming presence that Malik couldn't help but notice. He stood for a moment and watched the old car disappear through the greenery. His phone began vibrating in his pocket. He thought he'd switched it off.

'Roman, wha gwaan?'

'Where are you cuz...things are hot, blud'

'I'm off duh endz, left yesterday afternoon.'

'Good thing you did, because you woulda been number one suspect, yuh get me. Anyway listen, the Fedz have arrested Sticky. Just thought I'd let you know. I'm gone, yeah.'

'Hold on -'

The phone went dead.

As he walked down the uneven path, Malik cursed under his breath, unhappy with the mud forming around his new trainers. He switched off the phone, regretting answering it. The lake soon came into view like an oversized oil painting. Malik stood still and took in the beauty as nature began playing in his ears. It sounded good, far more soothing than his diet of grime tunes. He looked across the vast sheet of water and could just make out a man fishing with his young son on the far bank. Malik observed their movement for a while. Thoughts of his own father came back to him. Other than his prison status, he didn't know too much about the man who had swept his mother of her feet but failed to catch her when she was falling.

Malik found a patch of grass under an old silver birch and sat down. A lone wood pigeon cooed from up in the branches. He glanced up, then opened his book. He skipped a few pages and found a poem:

Product

I'm a lone soldier trapped in the greyness of deprivation
Bleakness coats the internal walls of my mind
Seducing me into a state of hopelessness
I search for myself, but myself I can't find.

Entrenched by flows of material dreams
My environment seemingly cursed by violence
How can I escape these walls of death?
When they've trapped me in and kept me silent

In this urban prison where I was systematically shaped
They banished me straight to the streets
Still they're feeding me politics like an edible substance
Now I'm sick to my stomach, how much more can I eat?

These walls of concrete are closing me in
Am I a product of this one directional system?
Will an environment determine my destiny?
Or will I change it and refuse to be a victim?

The words hit him, almost as if they had jumped of the page. He began to reflect on the streets of London. He inhaled the country air, the smell of damp tree bark and wild flowers teased his nostrils. Since arriving in Kent he hadn't heard a police siren and began to wonder if crime existed in the aptly named Garden of England. If it did, it didn't seem to show. The sound of footsteps crunching through the dry leaves got Malik's attention. *This must be Bradley*, he thought as his eyes set upon a stocky black man dressed in green combats, green vest and a khaki cap. His thick arms were full of equipment as he appeared from the pathway and approached Malik.

He smiled.

'Wha gwaan? You must be Malik, because there ain't any other explainable reason why a black yout would be sitting out here reading a book.'

Malik smiled pleasantly.

'Yeah Boss, fi real. It's nice out here man.'

Bradley touched fists with him.

'Come, we're gonna do some fishing.'

Malik grinned.

'Fishing? I ain't ever done fishing.'

Bradley shook his head, unsurprised.

'That's because your mind has been conditioned to think one way.'

'Wha you mean by dat, Boss?'

Bradley didn't answer; his mind seemed to be trapped in a zone. Malik studied him. He could already sense that he was deep; on another level. He was short and muscular with a clean bald head. His protruding eyes and hardened features showed all the signs of a man who'd lived life. Malik couldn't stop himself thinking that he was missing out on something, but he was not sure what.

They walked for a further 50 yards and then stopped at a clearing between two large trees. Bradley pulled a large backpack off his broad shoulders and placed it on the ground.

'Right, dis is us until tomorrow.'

Malik furrowed his brows.

'Until tomorrow?'

Bradley grinned mischievously.

'Yeah, until tomorrow. We are fishing and camping right through the night. Let's call it reuniting with nature. A ghetto detox.'

Malik glanced across the lake to a small island that was alive with birds of all species. A large greyish bird caught his eye as it descended to scoop a silver fish off the surface. He studied it closely, admiring its wing span.

'What bird's dat boss?'

'Bradley shielded his eyes from the sun that was now bursting through the clouds.

'That's a heron,' he replied

Malik watched the bird glide gracefully across the water with the fish firmly in its beak. He felt a spell of freedom for the first time in his life; it was almost too surreal to believe.

Apart from the odd ripple on the surface, the water was calm and quite clear for the time of year. Bradley took two fishing rods out from his holdall and handed one to Malik, who was still taking in the scenery.

'I can see you like it out here.'

Malik looked at Bradley as if he'd said something offensive.

'Wot? I love it out here. It's like I don't have to prove nuthin' and watch my back. Yuh get me.'

Bradley sighed deeply.

'Malik, that's how they've got you – The next yout is not your enemy – he wants to live, just like you.

'You see this right here? ...'

Bradley held his hands out.

'The trees, the birds, the lake ... this is God's artwork. No artist, not even Leonardo Da Vinci could create this masterpiece...'

Malik nodded slowly in admiration.

'Yuh see that grey prison you call home. That's man's artwork, designed to keep you in a defeated state of mind. You think it's a coincidence that mainly black people and uneducated white people are packed up in these estates like mice? The trap has been set - But hear what; clever mice avoid traps. Sometimes it just takes a trip to a place like this, to trigger a bit of meditation to make you see the whole lying picture that they sold to you in a concrete wrapping.'

Malik swallowed Bradley's words like edible gold. He vaguely remembered what Ronnie the Rasta man had said to him when he'd left prison. Something about mental slavery, he recalled.

Bradley seemed upset about something; he'd stopped talking and began to unravel the tent to set up for the night.

'Malik, I'm not gonna spoon feed you. You work out the rest for yourself.'

Grabbing some tent poles, Malik offered some assistance. He wanted to hear more, but Bradley had shut up shop for the day. Something had pissed him off.

When Lenny had called him and told him about Malik, he was apprehensive and wary. He'd moved down to Kent from South London and had never returned, apart from a flying visit every weekend to pick up his daughter. Leaving the city had become a necessity after living in the Caribbean for two years as a teenager. He'd found himself unsettled in London and after an unfortunate incident he seized the opportunity and left.

Malik sank back on a folded chair that Bradley had given him. They sat in silence watching the rods, waiting for a bite. He wondered what had pissed Bradley off. The sun was reflecting off the surface. Malik watched a cluster of tiny flies dancing by the water's edge. He couldn't help thinking that they had no idea what was going on.

'Yo, wake up bredrin. Yuh dreaming.'

Bradley nudged Malik, jumping him from his sleep.

'What, aye … wha gwaan.'

Malik sat up, still encased in his sleeping bag. He strained to focus and took a while to realise that he was still in a tent.

'Here, drink this.'

Bradley handed an enamel cup which was oozing with a minty fragrance.

'You're talking in your sleep. I don't know what's going on, but something's troubling you.'

Bradley wiped his hand across Malik's forehead.

'Look you're sweating.'

Malik sipped from the cup, collecting his thoughts.

Malik finished the drink and then climbed out of the tent. It was still early and the sun had barely risen.

'Look, I need to go yeah. Thanks and dat for everything … I learnt a lot out here man. But I gotta sort out something.'

Bradley watched Malik closely. He had empathy for him. He knew how hard it was for a young black man to make sense of the world around him. He could see that Malik was searching for something.

Malik deleted all the messages from his phone; he wanted to remain unreachable and disconnected for a while. He didn't want to think about London and whatever episode was kicking off. It was likely that violent flames would reignite between the Milly

Boys and D.O.A. Ninja's death would almost certainly spark retaliation. He'd texted Kia, his mother and Lenny to tell them he was ok. They were worried and he knew it, but things far deeper were haunting him deep in the darkest corridors of his mind.

He dug in his jacket for the business card that was given to him the day before. Finishing his cigarette, he dialled the number and waited.

'Hello, Tom speaking.'

'Tom, it's me, Malik ... duh black yout yuh met duh other day.'

Tom chuckled.

'Yes, I know who you are...what can I do for you?'

'Erm ... I need to talk and dat. But not on duh phone.'

Tom's voice took on a serious tone.

'Ok listen ... walk down to the bus station and jump on a 155 to Maidstone. When you get there, walk over the bridge and you'll see the Riverbank Bar overlooking the River. There's a small beer garden outside ... meet you there in about an hour. You got that?'

'Yeah, ok. Thanks.'

Sipping his beer, Malik observed the passengers queuing for a river boat. Kia would love this, he thought. He spotted a black couple strolling hand in hand. How they'd ended up in Kent he didn't know.

Maybe they were running from something too. Reflecting on what Bradley had said, he decided that maybe it was just their choice. Tom was late but it was ok, it gave him time to settle his nerves.

'Young man, how are you?'

Malik turned around to see Tom standing tall with a fresh glass of orange juice in his hand. He sat down at the table.

'You ok?'

'So-so…thanks for coming.'

Tom gazed into Malik eyes. They looked vacant.

'What's troubling you Malik?'

Malik stared at his glass, his head down almost in shame.

'I don't know where to start.'

Tom rested his hand gently on Malik's forearm.

'Start at the beginning.'

Malik slowly looked up, he looked uncomfortable.

'Is dis God business for real?'

'Why do you doubt that he's real?

Malik sipped his drink.

'I used to, but now I'm kinda thinking differently. It's like I was sent down here for a reason.'

Tom listened attentively.

'It's like my whole mind has just opened up. I was at the lake, remember, where you dropped me off. It almost felt like I was in heaven looking down at my own life. Everything just came to me proper vivid. I'm like, hold on … I should be dead right now.

Just near misses and somehow not being there when I was supposed to be there - yuh get me?

Tom's mobile began ringing. He switched if off.

'I'm listening.'

Malik paused, his head dropped.

'Tubbs,' he whispered before looking back at the pastor.

'My good fren died man, he ain't coming back. He turned and looked across the river, partly to focus on something else, partly to mask his emotions.

Tom watched Malik closely and sorrow began to fill his own eyes; he'd heard so many similar stories. He gave him a moment before speaking.

'Young man, you're feeling this way because God is awakening you. Can't you see? All this is not a coincidence. Think about it.'

'I have been thinking about it and everything makes sense to me now. I've been caught up in dis lie that us black youts are no good and we can only expect to be criminals, do sport or die on the street like dogs. Maybe God's got some plan for me, but I don't know because ...'

His voice trailed off, as he slowly shook his head.

Tom felt a deep sense of burden coming from the young man in front of him.

'Whatever it is, you need to release it.'

Malik looked up. Tears began to well in his eyes.

'I killed someone.' A lone tear found its way down his face.

Tom was not shocked; he half expected it.

'It's that murder that was on the news recently isn't it … in Hackney? His dad is a known criminal or something.'

'Yeah, Nathan Lewis. It was self-defence though, man. He came for me, it was self defence man'

'It's ok, just tell me what happened?'

Malik released a puff of air.

'Basically, he got a strap, you know, a gun. I got a call saying he was coming for me. So I ducked out to come to Kent to avoid him until things calmed down. My mentor was trying to squash things, but Nathan wasn't having it.

Anyway, I was on the train talking to my girl and he came through on her line, saying how he's coming round to do her something. I wasn't even clocking that he was baiting me, so I jumped off the train at Bromley South and jumped in a black taxi. The Blackwall tunnel was clear, so I got there pretty quick. When I got to my girl's block he was there waiting for me innit. He started gassing - I mean, talking bare madness in my head - about my girl and how I got him locked up. Then he drew the gun on me … But I was on him quick and we were tussling. The gun went off, innit. It's only when I got down here and switched on my phone that I heard he was dead.'

Malik broke down. His lips began to tremble.

'God ain't forgiving dat … trust me.'

Tom placed a calming hand on Malik's shoulder.

'God always forgives. Don't you see? As horrendous as this whole thing is, He still protected you from death.'

Malik wiped his face with the sleeve of his sweatshirt.

'I'm sorry man ... I don't usually cry for nuthin.'

'Crying is a great healer my friend. Just let it out. There's no shame in it.'

Tom waited for Malik to gather his composure.

'Malik, you need to hand yourself in. You can't run forever.'

'I know, I just don't wanna leave here right now.'

'Malik, you can be the change. I bet a lot a people look up to you. You've that warrior spirit about you.'

'Yeah, I suppose they do. Look, I'm gonna head back to the B&B, dis talking has drained me out. I need to lie down for a bit.'

Tom put his hand into a carry bag he was holding.

'Here's, a present for you.'

He passed Malik a brand new bible, encased in a cream gift box with a gold ribbon.

'God is setting you free.'

Malik shook Tom's hand tightly. 'You might see me in yuh church one day,'

Malik jested, but he was half serious.

Malik twisted restlessly on the bed. Although he felt tired he couldn't fall asleep. The B&B room was warm and stuffy. He'd finished all his cigarettes, but was in no mood to walk half a mile to the shops. He battled with the thought of giving himself up. Whispers from the street teased his already conflicted mind. A voice echoed in his head.

How can you snitch on yourself, blud?

He struggled hard to dismiss it, when suddenly the bedroom door violently burst open.

'Armed police...get on the floor *nooooow.*'

Shocked, Malik rolled off the bed and hit the deck. A heavy officer planted his full weight on his back; he could see and feel gun barrels pointing in his face. He waited anxiously to be read his rights - he was used to it - but nothing could prepare him for this one.

'Malik Simms...I am arresting you on suspicion of the murder of Nathan Lewis. You do not have to say anything, but it may harm your defence if you do not mention when questioned, something you may later rely on in court. Anything you do say may be taken down and given in evidence...Do you understand?'

Aftermath

It had rained relentlessly for the whole morning, dampening an already sombre occasion. The funeral cars had arrived early and were double parked in the road. Claudette adjusted her black dress in the mirror and redid her makeup for the third time, after another flow of tears. A lethal concoction of trauma and anger was poisoning her already fragile state. Downing another *Baileys* she slipped into her shoes. As she looked back in the mirror, standing there was Baron. So embroiled in her own emotions, she hadn't heard him come into the room.

'Yuh aright?'

Claudette angrily snapped her head around.

'Excuse me ... am I alright? You sick bastard, how could I be alright? Case you ain't noticed, we just lost our son. Remember Nathan, your mini you?'

Baron kissed his teeth.

'Yuh tink mi nuh feel pain too? Mi supposed to deh ah Jamaica now. Now mi haf fi fine who kill mi yout. He held up his right hand in the shape of a gun.

'Dead, whoever kill Nathan... *dead*, yuh hear me.'

Claudette screamed,

'What's wrong with you?! You're just evil. Nathan didn't have a chance with you around him. Now

you're talking about more killing on the day of

his funeral … you make me sick. Get out my room!'

Baron walked up behind her and placed his hands on her shoulder blades.

'Claudette, calm down nah…'

'Get ouuutttt!' she screamed.

Baron lifted his hands off her and left the room. Nathan's grandmother, auntie and a few other relatives were milling around in the kitchen. They stopped talking as Baron passed the door; they hated him and had done from the beginning. He fixed his dark glasses and made his way through to the conservatory. Sighing, he took his mobile phone from his back pocket and called Victor, his close associate.

'Victor, wha gwaan? Yuh find out anyting.'

'Yeah, some youts on that Howberry Estate; told me duh Fedz arrested a yout called Sticky.'

'But wha bout dis Malik boy?'

'He's disappeared, people are saying, he wasn't round duh endz when it happened. I don't know, bredrin.'

'He mus haf sumting to do wid it…look whoever kill mi boy, ha fi dead. Simple.'

Victor paused, contemplating.

'Baron…think dis thing through yeah. Remember Tony wants his gear back…and he dun warn you not to touch dat yout. You should just bury yuh son and go back to Jamaica bredrin … I'll keep duh business running. Don't watch that.'

Baron kicked over a wicker chair.
'Did your son dead?
'No he didn't, but -'
'But nuttin ... Nathan was my bwoy.'

After locking up the betting shop, Jennifer put the keys into her handbag. Looking up and down the High Road, she contemplated whether to go home or visit Lenny and Marcia. There was nothing at home, just a cold and empty flat. She looked forward to prayer meeting at the end of the week; just to feel the warmth of her church sisters. They'd prayed relentlessly for Malik's freedom the previous week. Placed on remand, Malik was locked up awaiting trial. He'd confessed to his mother over the phone that he had to survive and that he had major work to do. She didn't quite understand what he meant, but somehow her son sounded different.

Jennifer glanced up at the town hall clock; it had just hit 9pm. A September breeze brushed her face as she walked down to the bus stop, deciding to visit Lenny and Marcia. A group of youths bowled out of a chicken shop, startling her into a state of panic. Preoccupied with their grease-filled boxes, they hadn't even noticed her cowering behind the bus shelter. Since Malik's arrest, she felt naked - a sense of being watched and scrutinised as she walked in public. The police hadn't offered her any protection against possible reprisals. They left her lingering on the edge, almost afraid of her own shadow.

Marcia had offered to represent Malik in court, free of charge. Jennifer was more than grateful for her generosity, as she couldn't afford a reputable barrister and Marcia was very good. In fact, she was everything that Jennifer wanted to be, as far as her career anyway. *I'll get there*, she thought as she boarded the bus. She'd tried to pick up where she left off and had started an Open University degree, but the finish line seemed to be moving away from her every time she got close to it. The work load at her day job had increased dramatically due to staff cuts. This had left her no other option but to take work home and interrupt her studies.

Jennifer stood outside Lenny's door, cold and agitated. Banging the door knocker for a second time, she waited. Lenny's Audi was outside. *He must be in*, she thought.

The front door soon creaked open and Marcia appeared in the doorway. She broke into a wide smile and tied her long dreadlocks into a loose knot.

'Jenny, hi. Come in.'

Jennifer stepped into the house.

'Thank you.'

She followed Marcia into the sitting room and sat in a small armchair in the corner. Lenny stirred on the sofa. He had dozed off.

'Who's that, babe? He murmured, still half asleep

'It's Jennifer; she's come to talk to you.'

Lenny sat up and reached for his glasses on the arm of the sofa. He acknowledged Jennifer with an uncomfortable smile.

'Hey, you ok?'

'So-so I tried to call but I couldn't get through ... I just needed to talk.'

Lenny coughed and cleared his throat.

'Switched off my phone, I got dis flu ... well *man flu*, as you lot call it.' He chuckled.

Marcia took off her blazer and sat down next to Lenny. She watched Jennifer as she sat playing with her fingers. Marcia broke the ice and offered her a drink.

Lenny leaned forward.

'How's Malik?'

Jennifer nervously bit the corner of her mouth.

'He's ok. He's adamant that it was self-defence and I believe him.'

Marcia soon returned with a glass of sarsaparilla and handed it to Jennifer. She turned down the TV.

Jennifer sat still, quietly fighting back tears; she'd cried enough over Malik.

Lenny spoke up.

'The police came here earlier, asking me a whole heap of questions. I told them I sent Malik to Kent to avoid Nathan. They told me he'd already admitted to being at the scene, but I kept to my story. I don't trust them. I thought that Sticky yout done it. It's crazy. I didn't even think Malik was in the picture. I mean Ninja had a whole heap of enemies ... could have been anyone really.'

Jennifer finished her drink and placed the empty glass on the coffee table. She sighed.

'Well unfortunately, it was my Malik...the worst case scenario.'

Marcia interrupted.

'Jenny, I will do everything in my power to get your son off...you don't deserve this. I'm still waiting for the forensic report; I can't see them finding Malik's fingerprints on the gun anyway. I mean, which murderer leaves his gun behind?'

Jennifer nodded slowly.

'Yeah, you do have a point. Just hope the judge sees it that way. I mean Kia, poor girl. She's called me every day and all sorts. She's not coping with it all. Angela's gone off the rails again. I mean she wasn't the best of mothers, but she has been trying lately.'

'Well, she did find Nathan, you know,' Lenny interjected. 'She practically watched him die. That would mess up anybody.'

Marcia shook her head despairingly.

'These kids just don't stop to think about the damage they leave behind. If Nathan had just left Malik alone, he'd probably be alive now.'

Lenny looked at the floor; he disagreed but kept his opinion to himself.

Jennifer wiped a stray tear from her eye.

'When this is over, I have to get out of this place. I don't feel safe around here. Every time I see a group of boys or a car driving behind me ... I'm petrified. Who knows what's going to happen? Nathan's friends have already been up in my house and the police ain't helping me. It's disgusting. I ain't got no man to protect me. What am I supposed to do - other than pray?'

Marcia walked over to Jennifer and began stroking her shoulder. 'I'm going to help you...too many people need Malik out here.'

Lenny stood up.

'Nathan's gone, his gang will probably just dissolve. He was the engine behind it and a vehicle can't work wid no engine. I'll keep my ears to the ground.'

'Why haven't you told him?' Angela shouted.

'Told who what?' Kia yelled back.

'Malik. Why haven't you told him about the phone calls you keep getting?'

'What's the point; he's not here now is he?'

Angela gave Kia a searching look.

'Those calls didn't have anything to do with Nathan, did they?'

Kia froze momentarily, then sprang up from the sofa.

'Look, I'm not arguing anymore. You're getting on my nerves.'

Angela pulled hard on the spliff that was burning in the ash tray.

'That was Nathan calling you, wasn't it? Answer, me Kia!'

Kia began to walk out of the room, shouting as she went.

'You sit there and bun your weed, Mum, that's gonna solve all the issues around here! I'm practically raising Daniel by myself now. Just leave me alone, yeah.'

She slammed the door.

Kia had long suspected that her mother was dabbling with crack cocaine, but this time she was sure. Confronting her was too much of a challenge; she had to think about protecting Daniel. Carl was back sneaking around the flat like a bad spirit. She'd thought about asking Jennifer if she could move into Malik's empty bedroom but she daren't go behind his back.

Angela got up, wrapping her dressing gown around her thin frame. She looked out of the living room window, trying to focus on anything other than the visions in her head. As hard as she tried, she could

only see Nathan's lifeless body lying on the cold concrete. *Oh my gosh, so much blood. Why me? I should have just stayed inside.* She quizzed herself, tormenting her thoughts with graphic images.

Turning from the window, she took her mobile out of her dressing gown pocket. Her body was aching, partly because she hadn't eaten a proper meal in weeks. Hesitating, she decided to call her dealer; the urge was too strong.

Broken Silence

The atmosphere in the police station made Terry feel uneasy. It was sterile, yet being there felt unclean. He'd driven 17 miles to Hackney; he wanted to come in person. It was not a conversation to have over the phone. He paced up and down by the front doors, his mind was telling him to leave and drive away, but his heart was telling him to do the right thing. He was an honest man with a deep conscience, living with what he knew was a cross he was not prepared to bear. He began to sweat with anxiety.

'Excuse me, Sir, are you ok? Can I help?' asked the front desk officer.

Terry took a deep breath and strolled across the foyer.

'Erm…I need to speak to someone in connection with the murder of that kid a couple of months ago.'

The officer couldn't hide her surprise.

'Oh, I see…do you mean Nathan Lewis?'

Terry looked all around before answering.

'Yeah that's the one.'

'Hold on please, I need to call the officer in charge of the investigation.' Picking up the phone, the

woman speedily dialled an extension and then jotted down something on a notepad.

'Sarg, it's Nita. Could you come to the front

desk please, there's a gentleman here with some information.'

After a short wait, a gentleman brought Terry through to a small interview room and sat down around a long grey table. Terry timidly looked around the scantily furnished room. *What am I doing here?* He felt criminalised, even though he hadn't committed a crime. The man adjusted his tie before stretching across the table to shake Terry's hand.

'Good morning, I'm DS Hilton. And you are?'

'Oh, I'm Terry Finch.'

'Right, before we start, are you willing to make an official statement?'

Terry sighed as the reality of what he was about to do dawned on him.

'That's why I am here ... I need to get this stuff of my chest.'

Hilton slipped a pair of reading glasses out from his shirt pocket and put them on. Terry sniffed as a strong scent of aftershave aggravated his nose.

'Right Sir, so you say you have information about the murder of Nathan Lewis.'

Terry sat forward.

'Information...that's an understatement, I saw the whole thing.'

Hilton peered over the top of his glasses, surprised at the revelation.

'Excuse me ... you're telling me you saw the

whole thing?'

'Yeah I did - the whole thing - and it still haunts me now.

'Ok stop there. We need to document this. This is extremely crucial evidence. Why didn't you come forward earlier?'

'I was terrified. You always hear about witnesses getting intimidated or done over. But I heard an appeal on the news the other night. I've been drinking and all sorts, trying to run away from it -'

'Ok, you're here now. You've done the right thing. I'm going to record your statement, if you don't mind.'

Terry sighed deeply.

'Do whatever you need to do'

M alik headed down the long corridor towards the visitors' hall to await Kia's arrival. It had been a tortuous three months since he'd seen her. He had a lot of unanswered questions, a lot of unsorted garbage to place on the table. The thought of a possible life sentence was a hard nut to swallow, so he pushed it to the darkest room in his mind and tried to forget about it. Here and now mattered. He had things settled so that he could live in some sort of harmony. Reading books had become a part of his daily routine. With the court date looming, he'd set his mind on freedom as a coping mechanism. It was easier to think of life on the outside, creating his own bubble with Kia and Daniel firmly in it.

Malik fixed his prison issued tracksuit and strolled confidently into the hall. His eye soon caught Kia's waving hand from a table in the far corner. He strolled over, his stomach knotted.

Kia got up to embrace him but Malik stopped her in her tracks.

'Hold on, where's my boy ... where's Daniel?'

'I didn't bring him ... I don't want him up in this place.'

'What yuh talking about, I'm up in here, innit.'

Malik was vexed; he couldn't sit down.

'Simms, keep it down,' one of the prison officers barked.

Malik ignored him.

'I don't believe it ... wot are you on Kia?'

Kia sat back down at the small table.

'Malik, sit down.'

She spoke in her soft voice, the one that always calmed him. Eventually he sat down, struggling to look at her.

'Is there anything you wanna tell me Kia?'

'What are you talking about Malik?'

He kissed his teeth.

'Stop playing games yeah and just tell me wha gwaan.'

Kia began to well up.

'Malik, you're scaring me ... what are you talking about?'

'Ninja...'

Malik spat the words across the table.

'How come my man had your number? And why was he gassing to me about sleeping wid you and how Daniel might not be my yout ... yeah, how come? Dat was his last words before man try tek my life. Why Kia ... why?'

Kia looked Malik dead in the eye. Her bottom lip began quivering.

'He raped me...ok? You happy? He raped me and threatened me for months to get rid of the baby...' Tears began to flow down Kia's flawless face.

'I've been scared, ok. I couldn't tell you because I knew what you would have done, and look what happened anyway...'

She paused to wipe her eyes.

'I didn't ask for this Malik. That stupid Aisha brought him around my house ... he got her drunk, she passed out on the sofa. Then Nathan just switched, it was like he was possessed. He was going on about how you took me from him and how he loved me. The boy was acting proper off-key. Then he put a knife to me and made me strip ... I couldn't stop him, Malik...'

Her voice filtered down to a whisper.

'I couldn't stop him.'

Malik tried to speak, but the words were failing him. He punched down on the table top.

The patrolling officer warned him for the second

time.

'Bastard. Dis ting has been mashing up my head for months. So, Daniel might not be my yout, is that what you're telling me?'

'I think he is ... in fact, I know he is.'

Malik looked straight at Kia.

'You're not sure, are you?'

'No, I'm not. I'm sorry. When you come out, we can find out. Malik, talk to me.'

Malik got up. His face fixed with an icy stare. 'Dat's if I come out, Kia.'

He turned and walked away without saying another word.

The End of a Crooked Road

Mocha Coffee Bar was oozing its usual tranquil ambience. A group of city workers were congregated around a small table in the corner, drinking lattes and conveying their own self-importance. Katherine ordered an espresso and a buttered croissant, then sat down in a plush red leather sofa at the far end of the upmarket coffee shop. She began browsing through the *Guardian*, feeding her appetite for what she was about to do.

A young waitress briefly took her attention away from the newspaper, as she placed a plate on the coffee table in front of her.

'Your croissant madam.'

Katherine gave her a warm smile.

'Thank you.'

'Would you like anything else?'

'Not right now, thank you … I'm waiting for someone.'

'Ok, just let me know madam.'

The young female, adjusted her short skirt and then disappeared to serve another table.

Katherine glanced at the time and then over at the door. *He's late,* she thought, sipping her espresso. She drifted back into the newspaper, slowly scanning the pages as she turned them. Her eyes stumbled upon a story written by a former University friend.

'Alison Myers,' she whispered, remembering the quiet girl who used to sit next to her during lectures. She read the headline: *Copping it with a Witness*. She delved into the story, mainly to tear it to shreds, but as she got deeper it got better. It was faultless, concise and brilliantly written. Ironically, it was about corruption in the police force. Katherine pursed her lips, nodding.

'I'm impressed…two page spread in the Guardian as well,' she murmured under her breath with a tinge of distaste. Admitting was painful and she was envious, even though the story gave her the confidence boost she most certainly needed. She'd been having an internal argument with herself for weeks, but no matter how hard she tried to remove the thought from her mind, she felt used and undermined. DCS Rogers had to pay, and she had to get paid and that was final.

Closing the newspaper, she fired up her iPad to check over her own story. She'd spent weeks writing it, deleting it and rewriting it. It had to be impressive, convincing. Most of all believable, it could make her career or send it tumbling into the gutter. It would put her father in the limelight for all the wrong reasons or the right reasons, depending on how you looked at it. But she didn't care, and in her mind he didn't care either.

A presence hovering over her got her attention. She looked up at what seemed like a never-ending pair of legs until her eyes met with the chest of a man in a grey sports jacket and a blue check shirt. His curly deep rust hair made his plump face look paler than it probably was. He half smiled, as if he was not quite sure of himself.

'Are you Katherine?'

Katherine made eye contact.

'Yes I am. And you must be...'

He leaned over to shake Katherine's dainty hand

'David...David Clarkson from the Daily Mail. Can I sit down?' He held up a cup and saucer. 'This coffee needs drinking...'

Katherine shifted across to the right to make room.

He sat down and got comfortable before slipping a small laptop out from its case. He turned to Katherine, who looked nervous.

'You sure you wanna do this?'

Katherine hesitated for a few seconds.

'Yep, I'm sure...let's do it.'

'So, briefly ... you're saying you have evidence on two bent police officers. And what are they doing exactly?'

Katherine cleared her throat and put her iPad down on the coffee table.

'Well, basically ... where do I start? Have you heard of a man named Barrington Lewis? He's a major player in the drug trade in North London. His son was recently murdered in Hackney. It was all over the London news, you must have seen it.'

David rolled his eyes upwards. 'Err, that name rings a bell ... hold on ... wasn't he the one who allegedly kidnapped and murdered that businessman's wife because he wouldn't pay up some money? He got off, didn't he? Yeah, a colleague of mine ran the story ... nasty piece of work.'

'Yeah, that's him...big, bad Baron. Nobody will testify against him. He's a bloody psychopath.'

David rubbed his hands together.

'So what are you telling me? These officers are in collusion with him? Letting him operate without interruptions, that sort of thing?'

Katherine half giggled.

'Yeah, and let's say there are a couple of offshore accounts getting a regular feeding. I've been secretly recording meetings with them. I helped them out on something, but they can't prove it. I've done a lot of editing ... if you know what I mean.'

David laughed.

'You're a sly fox ain't you? Isn't your father Charles Peterson, Labour MP?'

'Yeah, unfortunately.'

'Well that explains everything. Crooked; it must be in your blood.'

Katherine went silent, not sure whether he was joking or deadly serious.

David eased the tension.

'I'm only joking luv. I thought you were going to walk out on me then.'

Katherine held her iPad up close to her chest.

'Before I go any further ... how much am I looking at for the story?'

David sat up to down his coffee, which was now stone cold.

'Ooh, we could be looking at six figures.'

Katherine's eyes lifted towards the ceiling. Her mouth opened.

'Six...'

Realising her own excitement, she promptly put back on her business face and tried to play it down. Yet inside she was dancing all the way to the bank.

With a couple of hours to kill before the end of their long shift, DS Thompson pulled the unmarked BMW out of the dead end street and then headed for Tottenham High Road. A deep fog had settled overnight, making it tricky to see up ahead. Thompson switched on the headlights and then wiped the inner windscreen with his shirtsleeve.

'Fancy a bit of fun?'

He grinned at Matthews in the passenger seat.

Matthews grinned back, in an unspoken agreement.

'What, a few stop and searches?'

Thompson nodded enthusiastically.

'Yeah, I fancy a bit of back chat.'

Matthews scoffed his bacon sandwich and threw the white paper bag out of the window. The weekend had been quiet so far. An informant gave them a tip-off about some potential gang activity. The intelligence had proven to be as hollow as the person it came from. Thompson drove the saloon slowly down the High road eying the shop doorways and alleyways, looking for someone's collar to ruffle. A monotone voice suddenly emerged through the receiver; they glanced at each other.

'All units, all units.'

Matthews promptly turned up the volume hoping to end the morning in a blaze of glory. The radio kicked back in. They both subconsciously leaned towards the dashboard: *'All units in the vicinity of the old Kestrel Industrial Estate N10...please attend immediately. Distress call put in by a member of the public...proceed with caution.'*

Matthews switched on the sirens, just as Thompson floored the accelerator, sending him flying back into the seat. Scrambling for his seatbelt, he secured his body and then sat tight.

'Right, let's see what we got ... better be good. It's been like a desert out here.'

Two buses up ahead swayed to the left as he slalomed in and out of the traffic at top speed, until the driver of a small green car, oblivious to the wailing siren, pulled out from a side road and screeched to a halt.

'Come *on* ... move, woman!'

Thompson yelled out of the open driver's window at the Nissan Micra that was now hogging the road. As he accelerated past, he gave a look that would have killed anybody, if they had dared look back. The BMW hugged the tarmac as they took the sharp bend into the disused industrial estate. Matthews cut the siren, vigilantly peering up and down the rows of metal grey units. Thompson slowed the car, straining to see through the grey mist that was still hovering.

'Hold on.' Matthews perked up. 'I think I saw something back there.'

Thompson hit the brakes and reversed backwards.

Matthews motioned his head towards some rusty shipping containers.

'There look! A bloke's waving down the end there.'

Matthews jumped out of the car and could hear a dog barking in the distance. Thompson switched off the engine and joined his colleague, who was now cautiously walking towards the commotion. A squad car screeched to a stop just behind them. The doors opened and two female officers appeared and joined them.

'What is it, Guv?' The shorter of the two asked.

'Not sure yet ...' Matthews replied.

An elderly man slowly hobbled towards them. He was clearly distressed and out of breath.

Thompson got to him first.

'Ok fella...what's the matter?'

The old man pointed to the side of one of the containers. His hand shook severely; something had rattled him. An old English bull terrier was barking erratically at the back doors of a burnt out van.'

'What, the van?' Matthews asked.

'Ye -yes... there's a -' he stuttered, pausing to regain his breath. 'There's a body in the back. Ma-ma ... my dog found it.'

'Are you sure?'

The elderly man adjusted his cheese cutter hat and nodded.

Matthews turned to the two female officers.

'Put him in the squad car. Poor bloke's freezing to death.'

Thompson had already run back to the car and returned with a couple of pairs of surgical gloves. He slipped on a pair and handed the other to his colleague. Once at the van, he waited for Matthews. Apprehensive, he grasped the half open door.

'Ok, here goes.'

He swung the door back, revealing a man's lifeless body. He'd been tied up and gagged. Thompson moved round to the side door to get a better view. It was still open. He noticed a single gunshot wound to his head, and then something more alarming.

'Oh shit! Matthews, come round here mate.'

He put his hand to his mouth and heaved.

Matthews moved quickly. He stood next to him, staring at the body.

'Is that who I think it is...?'

Thompson slowly lowered his head.

'Yeah mate. Baron. He's been tortured and shot, by the look of things.'

They both slowly moved away from the van. They'd seen enough. Thompson took his mobile out from his shirt pocket and began walking around in a wide circle before dialling.

'DCS Rogers'

'Guv, it's DS Thompson...'

'Thompson...I'm in a meeting, what is it?'

'Oh, I think you'll want to hear this...'

'What is it?'

'It's Baron - He's dead.'

There was a long pause.

'Bloody hell.'

Thompson could hear faint voices in the background. Then the phone line went dead.

Redemption Song

Malik clenched his fists tightly at his sides, thinking that if he squeezed hard enough, he could prevent the judge from taking his life out of his hands. He was desperate, trying every natural and supernatural gesture to prevent him from being sent down. His mind repeatedly played back the last two years of his life, like a video recording stuck on rewind.

Glancing around the courtroom, his eyes momentarily settled on Kia and his mother. They were huddled closely together; he'd never seen them that close before. His stomach twisted inside. *What if I go down?* The horrible thought stained his mouth with bitterness.

Terry the cab driver, that had bought Malik to Hackney that night, had just left the witness stand. He had given a blinding account of what he saw, despite the defence trying to back him into a corner. Malik watched him slowly leave the court in disbelieve. His picture of what he thought an Angel looked like; didn't look anything like Terry.

The judge peered down over his thick framed glasses at Malik as if he'd already tried, convicted and hung him from the nearest tree.

'Will…the…defendant…please…rise?'

His monotone voice sent ripples through Malik's body. He rose slowly, glancing around for the second time - this time at Lenny, who was sitting up in the gallery all suited and booted. Lenny raised his fist and then gently tapped it against his chest. He mimed something, which Malik interpreted as *One Love*.

Marcia stood close by, her long locks almost blending into the back of her black barrister's gown. She looked the part and had played it well too. Her performance was more than impressive, in fact it was sublime.

It was quite evident that the snobbery of the opposing barrister had grossly underestimated her, allowing his prejudice and preconceptions to overshadow his professionalism. She had firmly put his nose out of joint. The clerk handed the judge the case notes, which he began summarising. Malik focused on a large plaque of the Royal Coat of Arms, which was securely fitted to rich mahogany panelling, just behind the judge's head. The plaque seemed to ooze a sense of superiority that had Malik concluding that the powers that be were against him.

Shutting down his emotions, he lowered his head and closed his eyes; he could almost feel the heartbeat of the gallery behind him. The judge adjusted his glasses and then passed the notes back to the clerk. Malik braced himself, praying for redemption under what felt like his last breath. A slim, well dressed lady of a Mediterranean appearance took her position, verdict in hand. The words seemed to take an age to leave her lips as she looked up to address the court. She cleared her throat.

'We the Jury...' she began. 'Find the defendant Malik Anton Simms ... *not guilty!*'

She didn't know whether to curse him and leave him on the doorstep or allow him in and see what he had to say for himself. Instead, Claudette said nothing and walked back into the house, leaving the front door wide open. Malik stalled on the doorstep, unsure. He began second guessing his thoughts until the decision was taken away from him.

'Come in then.' Claudette shouted from in the depths of the house.

Malik straightened his jacket and wearily made his way down the corridor, stopping to observe a portrait of a young Nathan on the wall. It was an old school photo, yet his eyes had the same dull glare of a boy with a painful story to tell. Malik let out a gasp of air and made his way towards the sound of a TV coming from the living room. .

Claudette quietly stood by the window, staring across the road, her back facing Malik.

'Sit down young man,' she said without turning around.

Malik glanced around the chic interior as he lowered himself into the sofa. He had imagined

Nathan to be living in a rundown council flat, not a spacious terraced house with Italian furniture and solid oak flooring. If drug money had a fragrance, Malik could smell it. Claudette soon turned around, arms folded.

'You've got guts; I give you that, coming to my house.'

Malik rubbed his two hands together, rehearsing the speech that was firmly in his head.

'I'm sorry, I had to come,' Malik paused.

His script vanished from his head, leaving him scrambling for words.

'I just, erm ... I don't know what I'm trying to say. What I wanna say is ... I'm sorry, yeah. Bout Nathan and dat ... I didn't mean for what happened. He tried to-'

'Look, I know ... you don't need to explain. I heard it all in court. I believe you.'

Malik looked up, half surprised.

'You do?'

'Yes I do. I know you're sorry. I could see it in your eyes. Nathan was heading in one direction. I just regret the day I met his father. I suppose you've heard he's been murdered.'

Malik nodded.

'Yeah I heard.'

Claudette exhaled, releasing some built up anger.

'Somehow, I can start to rebuild my life. I will always miss Nathan. As for Barrington, I hope he *burns* in hell.'

Malik looked into her eyes; he could see rage mixed with pain. He waited for her to elaborate, but she didn't.

'All I wanted to ask you, Miss Lewis-'

'Miss Knight,' she corrected him. 'Lewis is that man's name. Just call me Claudette.'

'Oh, sorry...' Malik paused for thought.

'I just wanted to ask you if you could forgive me for what happened. I'm really trying to change my life. I need to bury certain demons. Yuh understand me?'

Claudette sat down next to him.

'Malik, isn't it?'

'Yeah.'

'I really appreciate you coming here. It shows you're willing to face up to things. We all need closure. I would have probably spent the rest of my life bitter and blaming you. When, in reality, Baron killed Nathan.'

Claudette's statement cut the conversation to shreds, leaving Malik feeling it was time to make his exit. He got up and thanked Claudette for her openness.

She opened the front door and let him out.

'Malik,' she called out.

Malik turned around.

'I forgive you.'

A New Dawn

— ❖ —

Kia gently placed the brown envelope down on the bed as if it contained enough explosives to blow up the whole block of flats. To Malik, it might just as well have been a letter bomb because what was inside could blow his heart into oblivion. He watched the envelope as if it was about to come alive.

'Well, who's going to open it?'

Kia placed her hands either side of her face, reading the address, over and over again.

'I suppose it's going to have to be me...'

Malik turned to face the bedroom door and placed his head into his hands.

'Go on, den.'

Kia apprehensively picked up the envelope and then slowly slid a long fingernail under the seal. Her heart thumped against her chest like a kicking unborn child. She lifted the flap and took the letter out. Malik covered his ears, putting a barrier between him and the result that could potentially reshape his life. A few seconds passed, but it felt like

five minutes. He felt Kia's finger prod into his rib cage, probing him to turn around. She was smiling like a child who had just received ten A-Levels.

'Wot?' he asked, half smiling.

Kia leaned forward, kissing him on the lips.

'He's yours Malik. Daniel's yours you idiot.'

Malik snatched the letter, glancing at Daniel, who was sleeping in his travel cot, before he read it.

'Right, can we move to Kent now?' Kia asked.

Malik grinned, he was elated.

'Hell yeah...standard.'

Kia threw her arms round his shoulders.

'Is this really you?'

Malik grasped her around the waist.

'Murkz is dead, trust me. I'm done wid dat life. I'm laying it all on the table. Me, you and little man ... fresh start.'

Kia puckered her glossy lips and gave him a longer taste of strawberry passion, looking longingly into eyes that had a shine that had long been missing. His eyes were no longer blood red and glazed; he hadn't pulled on a stick of herbs for months, choosing to read the bible and finish the book Lenny had given him.

Malik pulled away from Kia's embrace and put his hand under his mattress.

'We can rent a flat,' he said, producing his stash of money. 'Duh deposit is right here, yuh get me.'

Kia's mouth slightly opened.

'What, where did you get that, or should I not bother asking?'

Malik squinted, shaking his head from side to side. Kia knew what that meant. *Don't ask questions.*

Daniel stirred and rolled over, briefly opening his eyes before drifting back to sleep. Malik watched him and then turned back to Kia.

'Why did you name him Daniel?'

'I named him after you, you fool.'

Kia playfully pinched his arm.

Malik's forehead crumpled with confusion.

'Aye...'

'Durrr...Daniel in the lion's den, bible story innit. That was you out there on road. You should have been *devoured*, but God was with you the whole time.'

Malik looked even more confused.

'But how did you know dat? You ain't spoken about God before.'

Kia curled her lips downwards, shrugging her petite shoulders.

'I didn't know...it just came to me innit.'

Malik looked up towards the ceiling.

'Dis ting is *deeeeep*.'

Kia stared at her man, not sure of what he was talking about, but she was sure he knew.

'**B**loody hell...sod living round here.'
     Tony eased the Audi R8 over another overly high speed hump, looking up at the decaying bricks that were holding the decrepit flats together. Strong reminders of the high-rise flats in Bethnal Green, where he grew up, sprang into his mind. But

that was a long time ago, an existence he had soon forgotten. He glided into a parking bay and then got out of the car, into the gaze of several eyes coming from a circle of purple bandanas. They'd come from nowhere. The black Audi was hardly inconspicuous; especially on a rundown estate like Howberry.

Tony withstood their stares, sensing that whatever they had in mind, they were having a rethink. He closed the car door and then turned his huge frame around to face them head on.

'Can I help you, lads? You look like you wanna say summink.'

The boys soon realised what day it was; it was not a day to be messing with the big guy. After a mumbling undertone, they turned to disperse.

Tony watched them with a chilling stare.

'That's it lads, jog along.'

Shaking his head he headed for the entrance to Shelton House. It was 10am, so he pressed the trade button. The door bleeped a long tone. Tony checked behind his back and then stepped into the block. After climbing the two flights of stairs, he soon located number 15 and clattered the letter box.

The door soon opened and a baffled Malik stood in the doorway.

'Rah ... Tony, what you doing here?'

'What do you mean, what am I doing here? Come to see you off, ain't I.'

Malik widened the door.

'Come in man.'

He followed Malik down to the living room, where Jennifer and Kia were packing Daniel's toys into a cardboard box.

'Mum, look who's here...'

Jennifer looked up and immediately worked out who the giant in the room was.

'You must be Tony.'

'Yeah luv, nice to meet you at long last. Your boy talks my ears off about you.'

Jennifer half laughed.

'Really?'

'Yeah, really. And you must be the gorgeous Kia.'

Kia raised a hand and gave a reserved wave.

'Hiya.'

Tony smiled, before turning to Lenny who was sitting on the sofa reading a newspaper. He had popped over to say his farewells.

'Here Len, I just saw Kermit and the rest of the Muppets downstairs.'

Lenny looked up from the newspaper, all too familiar with Tony's sense of humour.

'You're talking about the Milly Boys.'

'Oh, is that what they're calling them nowadays?'

Lenny laughed, but he could see a hint of empathy in Tony's eyes.

Tony looked towards the window.

'Jokes aside, they looked like a bunch of scared kids with no hope. Quite sad really.'

'Tony, have you read this?' asked Lenny, holding up the front page of the newspaper.

Oh what, front page...*Daily Mail*? Yeah I read it mate...more bent coppers. That journalist fitted them up good and proper. It seems like they had Baron under the cosh.'

Lenny continued reading.

'It says here, DCS Rogers has fled to Brazil. They're trying to get him extradited. Makes you wonder if they had anything to do with Baron's murder.'

Tony shrugged his huge shoulders.

'Maybe or maybe not. Who knows?'

A horrible thought registered in Lenny's head, it was clear and vivid.

Tony turned away and focused back on Malik.

'Erm, where's the kitchen mate? I wanna quick word.'

Malik ushered Tony into the small kitchen and shut the door. A million questions flooded his mind, knowing that when Tony wanted a word, it was either business or some strong words.

'Relax mate ... I'm a bringer of good tidings.'

Malik frowned.

Tony pulled a set of keys out from his jacket pocket and held them out on his upturned index finger.

'Right, I've got a nice little two bedroom house in Maidstone; overlooking Moat Park Lake. It's yours, if you want it. You ain't gotta pay me any rent for the first year - give you some time to sort yourself out. You've got a lovely young lady out there and a cute little boy. You kids need a chance. I don't know if I'm turning soft or what, but I wouldn't wanna hear that you got killed over some bollocks. Here ... take um.'

Tony put the keys into Malik's hand. 'I'll text the address to your phone. Now go and tell your girlfriend, she's a good one, mate. Don't mess it up.'

Malik vigorously shook Tony's hand.

'Thanks, Boss. I ain't gonna forget this.'

'You can thank Lenny as well. He told me you loved it down there. I've got properties all over the gaff. Now go on; we'll talk about your job and that later.'

'Is yuh mum gonna be alright?' Malik asked Kia.

'She's gonna have to be - I'm not gonna miss this opportunity.'

'Yeah fi real. She can come and visit anyways.'

Kia nodded in agreement.

'I suppose so...I'm gonna miss Aisha though. She's being released from prison next week.'

Malik put his last pair of trainers into a black bin liner and scanned the open wardrobe.

'But I have to come back down here still; even if it's every other weekend...I wanna do something. Talk to the road youts and try to make some changes, yuh get me. We've been hoodwinked man. It's not all about where we live - it's the environment in our heads that needs changing…'

A soft knock on the bedroom door intruded on the conversation.

'Come in,' said Malik.

Jennifer popped her head around.

'Pastor Denton's here. He wants to pray with you guys before you leave tomorrow.'

'Ok, we're coming.'

They marched out into the living room; where the Pastor was sitting up straight enjoying a coffee.

'Good evening, young man and young lady. I hear that you're leaving us.'

Malik placed his clenched fist into his other hand.

'Yeah, need a fresh start, a change of scenery,'

'Well, you couldn't have chosen a better place. Most of Kent is beautiful. God definitely painted a few pictures down there.'

Kia smiled, hearing the confirmation.

Pastor put his cup on the coffee table and then got up.

'Ok, let's join hands.'

Jennifer joined in to complete the circle.

'Let's bow our heads,' he began. 'Father God, we come to you for your guidance and *protection* over this young family - Malik, Kia and young Daniel. I pray for your grace and mercy to reign over them as they venture out into a new beginning. Malik has been running for so long, trying to make sense of this world. *Evil* has come to him in many forms.

But because of your mercy, it has not prevailed. His mother, Jennifer, has continued to pray for him, that one day he would see the light. Now I ask you Lord, to go with them on this journey, encourage them to live a righteous life. Watch over them, day and night...we thank you in advance. Amen.'

'Amen,' they all said. Malik kept his head down trying to disguise the lone tear that had made its way down his face.

Pastor placed a gentle hand on Malik's shoulder.

'Don't fight it son ... let it go.'

Malik looked up slowly.

'Dis is gonna sound dumb, but I wanna give my life to God.'

Jennifer looked up, struggling to contain her tears. She had suffered long for this day; fasted, cried and prayed.

Pastor guided Malik to the other side of the room for a bit of privacy.

'Young man, you are making the biggest and best decision in your life, but I must warn you to be on your guard. Everything will come to throw you off track. Do you understand me?'

Malik nodded, he was ready, no matter what. He knew God was calling him, he had been for a while. For the first time in his life he felt like there was a reason for his existence.

Pastor opened the bible and searched for an appropriate scripture. Malik closed his eyes remembering a dream he had in prison. He was standing at a major junction with a suitcase full of burdens. To his left was a wide road full of city lights, but seemed to be heading nowhere in particular. On his right was a narrow winding path and at the end of the path he could see a single flashing light, almost like a lighthouse in the middle of a dark sea. He could remember smiling figures, drenched in gold, enticing him down the wide path, promising him all the riches he could possibly imagine.

Then an almost silent whisper came from beyond the flashing light, beckoning him to come forward. It was the guard's keys rattling on the door that had woke him up and reminded him that he was locked in a 6 x 6 prison cell. Pastor Denton located the scripture and then instructed Malik to repeat after him.

Ten month old Daniel ran unsteadily through the open plan living space, chasing his ball. His pink tongue hung from his dribbling mouth, as he enjoyed the freedom. Kia stood by the patio doors admiring the compact back garden. Apart from the need of a grass cut, it was neat and well maintained with a yellow and blue plastic slide, which sat next to a tree swing. To the left of the garden was a mini waterfall, trickling down into a small pond. Along the garden fence were trimmed rose bushes and shaped hedges. She smiled, thinking back at the many days she'd spent in her Hackney bedroom daydreaming about such a garden. It was almost picture perfect; the house was just as lovely with natural wood floor throughout and a modern fireplace. Malik busied himself in the kitchen unpacking the crockery that his mother had brought as a going away present.

The black granite worktops and white gloss cupboards oozed quality, reminding him of Tony's expensive taste; he didn't expect anything less. A Chronixx tune rumbled through his phone earpiece, putting him on a natural high as he worked his way through the boxes. He suddenly remembered the bag of cash which was now surplus. Removing it from his coat pocket, he shoved it into an old biscuit tin and hid it at the back of one of the cupboards. He thought about buying Kia a new car. His phone began ringing, cutting into his favourite tune.

He answered reluctantly.

'Hello, who dis?'

There was a long silence at the other end of the line, but he could feel an atmosphere and heard faint noises in the background.

'Hello, I ain't got time for no games. Who dis?'

'Hello, Malik, it's me...Zoe.'

'Rah, Zoe. You've been missing. I thought you were in Spain.'

'I am in Spain. Didn't Tony tell you?'

Malik kicked the kitchen door shut.

'Yeah...he said you were sorting out your dad's

new club, but I thought you were back.'

'Well, that ain't entirely true…. My dad sent me out here because…' she paused.

Malik became agitated.

'Because what?'

'…because I've had a baby…a little girl … She's yours.'